Yellow flames flickered in the fireplace, woodsmoke filled the room and for a moment Emily thought someone was watching her.

A shadowy figure stepped away from the bookcase. Big. Tall. And dressed as a British redcoat.

"Wh—" The word couldn't get past the lump in her throat. She tried again. "Wh-who are you?"

"Captain Calvert T. Witherspoon, at your service, madam." He swept off his tricorn hat and bowed. "You should be asking yourself how I arrived here in your parlor."

"I left the front door unlocked?" She eyed him with a mixture of surprise and anxiety.

"Unnecessary, I assure you." He looked so smug, she wanted to scream. "I merely walked through the wall." And, placing his hat firmly on his head, he bowed once... and in three steps vanished into the bookcase.

ABOUT THE AUTHOR

For Charlotte Maclay, a little article buried inside the newspaper or the people she knows are unending sources of book ideas. Charlotte's inspiration for *A Ghostly Affair* was a very simple theme: Love is what makes us human. "I had great fun writing this book," she says. "When two people belong together, the magic of love conquers all."

Books by Charlotte Maclay

HARLEQUIN AMERICAN ROMANCE
474–THE VILLAIN'S LADY

CHARLOTTE MACLAY

A GHOSTLY AFFAIR

Harlequin Books

TORONTO • NEW YORK • LONDON
AMSTERDAM • PARIS • SYDNEY • HAMBURG
STOCKHOLM • ATHENS • TOKYO • MILAN
MADRID • WARSAW • BUDAPEST • AUCKLAND

Published May 1993

ISBN 0-373-16488-2

A GHOSTLY AFFAIR

Chapter One

The racket outside startled him awake.

With a mumbled curse, Calvert T. Witherspoon, late of His Majesty's service, rolled off his bed and staggered across the room. His stockinged toe stubbed against an eighteenth century Queen Anne rocking chair that had been stored in the attic for more than two hundred years.

Hopping on one foot and rubbing his toe, more from habit than pain, he muttered another oath. "Why can't these bloody colonials leave a man to rest in peace?"

He pulled back the lace window curtain an inch or two. The dormer window gave him a view of the yard, a grassy patch surrounded by the bright autumn colors of a New Hampshire afternoon.

With a dark frown, he studied the scene.

A ragtag mob had gathered on the circular carriage path below him—people and those noisy, smelly machines they were so proud of. Clearly these Americans were too ignorant to realize their new-fangled invention reeked of noxious fumes as badly as the entire town of Liverpool had, last he'd visited there. Which, he conceded, had been some time ago.

A woman appeared to be organizing the motley crew. She'd been here before, albeit briefly, he recalled. Her familiar voice—a clear, soft soprano—drifted up to his open window. As she gave a series of quick orders, her hands moved in graceful arcs, rather like dancing girls he'd known, who were now only memories from his distant past.

Ah, the London theatres, he thought with a sigh. So glorious. And the ladies so willing.

Though the woman he observed had the moves of a dancer, her blond hair was decidedly dreadful. It was shorn, Lord help him, shorter than that of most men he'd known. He'd always preferred his ladies to have long, golden locks with honeyed strands that he could lace his fingers through, or feel draped across his chest during those delightfully intimate moments when he had—

Abruptly, he cleared his throat and scratched at his unkempt beard. No cause to dwell on a part of the past that was no longer available to him.

The sound of childish laughter drew his attention to the far side of the yard.

A wee little lass with long, blond hair the same shade as her mother's pursued an equally fair-haired boy around an ancient maple tree. Their racing feet threw up an array of red and gold leaves from the ground, and giggles lifted in a guileless duet. Finally the lad relented, turning from his easy escape to catch up his sister in midstride. He awkwardly carried the child back to their mother's side. Without missing a beat with the workmen, the mother managed to give each of her children an affectionate caress.

Calvert scowled. It was clear a mother and her two children were about to invade his domain. A new stove had appeared out of a motorized carriage, and boxes and valises were being hauled inside in a steady stream. But what of a husband?

He scanned the area once more. The males appeared to be no more than hired workmen. Some he even recognized as colonials who lived in the community.

Interesting, he mused. Not that a woman with only her children for protection would change his plans.

Every thirty years or so, some brave soul had decided to inhabit Henderson House—a haunted house, by all local accounts. He'd driven each interloper off for the last two hundred years, or thereabouts.

Naturally, Calvert T. Witherspoon, second son of the distinguished Lord Albert Witherspoon, and Captain in His Majesty's Own, would do the same with these new arrivals. It never took long.

EMILY ALICE BARTON Morrell checked off box number twenty-three on her clipboard. Contents: silverware and everyday dishes.

"That one with the red stripe goes in the kitchen," she told the burly moving-van driver as he slid the dolly under the box. If she and the kids were going to eat tonight, she'd have to get that container unpacked first.

"What aboot the blue-striped 'uns, ma'am?" his young assistant asked, his New England accent as thick as the last dregs of maple syrup in a pot.

She glanced at her list. "Blue is for Peter's room. Upstairs. Second door on the right."

"I'll show him, Mom. Can I?"

"All right, son, but don't get in his way."

"Me, too! Me, too!" echoed four-year old Rebecca.

Emily caught her daughter's hand before she could race up the porch steps after Peter. "No, Becky, you stay out here with me. You can tell me what color the stripes are on the boxes so the men will know where to put them."

Becky didn't look at all convinced the task was worthy of her attention. Chasing after her big brother clearly held far more appeal, even at the risk of being trampled by the movers.

Sighing, Emily pulled the child close up against her jean-clad thigh and hugged her. Organizing a cross-country move was easy compared to keeping up with two energetic youngsters. If Emily Morrell was anything, she was certainly well organized and thoroughly logical. Planning her way through myriad details was a piece of cake for a former computer programmer.

What she lacked, however, was a couple of extra sets of arms and legs, and eyes in the back of her head to keep track of Pete and Becky. A husband would have been helpful in that regard, she thought, the dull ache of widow's grief tugging in her chest. After three years it still felt like she'd swallowed an indigestible rock whenever she allowed herself a moment to think about Ted.

When a car slid into a spot on the gravel drive behind the moving van, Emily looked up from her clipboard. Forcing a smile, she watched as Brady Berrington climbed out of his pristine Cadillac. The plaque attached to the car door identified Brady as representing Honorville Realty, N.H. He and his father had managed the Henderson property for years while the owners remained absentee.

"Hiya, Emily," he said, the cool breeze lifting his thinning hair. "Everything going okay?"

"So far, so good, if you don't count a smashed lamp shade as a disaster."

"Guess you have to expect that sort of thing," he agreed.

Brady had that long, angular look that reminded Emily of the Disney version of Ichabod Crane. "Nice of you to drop by."

"Well..." He dragged out the word. "I worry about you out here all by yourself with the nearest neighbors more than a stone's throw away. Henderson House hasn't been lived in for, uh, maybe thirty years. If it gets to be too much for you..." Letting the words hang, as though some ax were about to behead her, he stared up at the dormer windows in the attic. "Folks do talk about..."

Emily's gaze followed his. A breeze shifted the window curtains and a strange coolness tickled the base of her spine. She ignored the sensation.

"Now, don't start giving me that ghost-story business again. Great-Aunt Minerva willed this place to me, and I intend to turn it into the finest bed-and-breakfast in all of New England." The house had been in the Henderson branch of Emily's family forever, though none of her relatives had ever lived here, as far as she knew. In her will, Minerva had stated that because Emily carried the family's traditional girl's middle name of Alice, she should be the one to inherit the house. The assorted cousins hadn't objected. Scattered across the country, Emily was the only Henderson offspring with any interest in the family ancestry. And the timing had been right.

"Just wanted you to know I'm here," Brady said. "If you need me for anything at all." He pointedly cocked his head in a knowing way and touched her lightly on the arm. "Or if you should decide to sell. I know women sometimes make hasty decisions, and this part of the country can be a bit hard on strangers."

Emily bristled. Brady was doing a male-female thing, as if he didn't believe she had good sense. Though it might appear to others she had made this move impulsively, that wasn't true. She'd done balance sheets and projections, talked to a half-dozen owners of B and B's in the area and arrived at her decision in quite logical fashion. She was sick to death of the pressures and long hours of the aerospace industry in California and needed a way to support herself while still having enough time to spend with her children. Henderson House made sense.

Once she made up her mind, she admitted, Emily Alice Barton Morrell could be downright stubborn. Must be her New England ancestry, she concluded as she stepped away from Brady's unwelcome touch. After all, Emily was a direct descendant of Alice Henderson Barton, who had once lived in this beautiful house.

"I assure you, the children and I will be just fine, and we have no intention of selling."

She had to give Brady credit. He left with a pleasant, if skeptical, smile and wishes for good luck.

By the time the movers had emptied the van and placed the contents more or less in the correct rooms, long afternoon shadows crisscrossed the yard.

"Come on, kids," Emily called to her children, rounding them up from where they'd been exploring the side yard. "I've got to run to the store. Into the car with you."

"Aw, Mom . . ." Peter complained.

She opened the car door for them. "It won't take long, and I know a couple of kids who won't be pleased if they don't have any food for dinner." Or milk for breakfast, she mentally added to her list.

From the corner of her eye, she caught a movement in the upstairs window again, the same curtain that had fluttered when Brady had been here. She shook off a repeat of goose bumps at the base of her spine. Deciding she'd have to make sure that particular window was firmly latched in the future, she slid into the car behind the steering wheel.

At the grocery store, Emily picked up only basic items to see them through the next day or so. Then, leaving the youngsters in the car, she parked in front of the Pierce Family Drugstore to pick up a birthday card for a friend in California. According to the sign hanging above the door, the business had been established in 1769. Indeed, the building had a musty smell that made the sign quite believable.

Making a quick selection, Emily carried the card to the cash register. A thin-lipped woman whose name tag identified her as Zella Pierce took the card from her hand.

"You that woman who's movin' into the Henderson place?" the woman grumbled.

"Why, yes...."

"You won't last long." The woman jabbed at the cash register with a bony finger.

Startled by the abrupt announcement, Emily forced a smile. "I plan to be here a long time, Mrs. Pierce. Hopefully, I'll even bring in some new business for your store." The economy in New Hampshire could use any boost it could get, and tourism was a big industry.

The old woman stared at her through inch-thick glasses. Hair that should have been silver-gray, based on the number of wrinkles crinkling her face, was an odd shade of blue.

Zella humphed. "We don't take much to folks from the outside comin' here to tell us how to run our business."

"I may have just arrived in town, but my roots in Honorville go back a long way, Mrs. Pierce. Before the Revolutionary War, as I understand it." Emily had hoped her new England ancestry would help her ease into the closed little community.

"You're a Henderson." She said the name as though identifying a large, black bug.

The smile on Emily's face faded. "I'm a direct descendant of Alice Henderson Barton, and very proud of my ancestry," she said tightly. It would take more than a few moments of pleasant conversation to turn Zella Pierce into even a cordial acquaintance. "If you'll just tell me how much I owe you?"

Paying with exact change, Emily hurried back to the car. What a strange way to welcome someone to the neighborhood, she mused.

HOURS LATER, Emily found her back was aching and her head throbbed. Moving was not an easy chore, she concluded. And she was a long way from being settled in.

Except for two hyperactive children still thundering up and down the curving staircase, the house was amazingly quiet after a dinner of soup and sandwiches. No doubt she'd lived too long within earshot of Los Angeles freeways to appreciate country silence. It seemed to press in around her, heavy and thick like a fog that had settled itself across the landscape. She strained to hear familiar sounds.

A car hummed by on the road two hundred yards in front of her house. In the distance, a cock crowed. Somewhere, a hammer clanged against metal.

As she stretched out a length of shelf paper across a kitchen cupboard, she decided living in the country was going to take a bit of adjustment.

EXCEPT FOR A FEW brief moments of peace and quiet when the trespassers had left the house, Calvert had been watching her all afternoon...her and those ragamuffin children. He wasn't used to all that screaming and commotion. His head felt like someone had been using it as an anvil; his mood had moved beyond surly.

Now that the children were in bed and the house finally quiet, he was ready to make his presence known. In no uncertain terms.

In the closet he found the heap of rusty chains he used. He planned to add a few well-timed moans and a fluttering white sheet. That ought to convince the lady in those rather enticing, tight-fitting trousers that she didn't belong in his house. Pity was, dressed in suitable attire, she'd be quite attractive. Slender waist. Adequate bust—more generous than that, he corrected—and the heart-shaped face of an angel. Already he'd become accustomed to the short halo of curls that managed to frame her face like a golden sunrise.

He imagined for a moment running his fingers through that hair, grabbing a handful to enjoy its texture and soft, silky strands. A pleasurable experience, no doubt.

And her lips, which formed readily into a quick smile, were nicely shaped, he decided, the lower one slightly pouty. Perfectly suited for a man to—

A pox on such nonsense!

He dragged one end of the thick chain from its hiding place. A trip or two down the stairs ought to be enough to frighten off the noblest of hearts. He straightened his red tunic and sword, then proceeded into the hallway.

THE FIRST SOUND gave Emily a start. Houses originally built in 1760 were bound to be filled with creaks and moans. That one had been a real humdinger. The foundation must be settling, she decided. It seemed reasonable the old structure would be making some adjustments, given the amount of activity it had endured all day.

Shaking her head, she unwrapped another plate from the packing carton and placed it on the stack to be washed.

Two heavy thuds followed a metallic clatter. Quite loud and decidedly inside the house.

The kids must have gotten out of bed. What on earth were they up to now?

Trying to muster some semblance of patience at the end of a hard day, she pushed out through the swinging kitchen door.

"Mommy! Mommy!" The pajama-clad youngsters raced barefoot down the curving staircase in tandem.

"What's wrong, Pete? What are you doing up? It's way past your bedtime." She cupped the back of her daughter's head. "Yours, too, Becky."

Peter's blue eyes were hugely round. "It's the ghost, Mom. We heard the ghost!"

Emily stifled a smile. Kneeling, she placed an arm around each of her children. "What you two heard were simply the sounds of an old house. We'll get used to them."

"But, Mom!" Peter objected, his voice high-pitched. "The mover told me the house is *haunted.*"

"That's just superstitious nonsense, honey. He was teasing you." Or for whatever reason, trying to frighten them off. So far, the townspeople hadn't shown a great deal of enthusiasm for Emily's arrival. "We're from California, and Californians do *not* believe in ghosts."

"Are you sure?"

"Absolutely positive." She took each of the children by the hand and marched them back up the stairs to their beds.

"DAMN HER EYES!" Calvert dropped the chains to the floor in disgust.

Not believe in ghosts? He'd show her a thing or two.

Chapter Two

She'd survived the weekend. Just. Three whole days in
this creaking, groaning house and Emily hadn't had a
full night's sleep yet. Little wonder she couldn't find
the strength to get up off the comfortable couch to go
up to bed. She'd just stay here a moment more, until
the fire in the lovely granite fireplace died down a bit.
The yellow flames flickered hypnotically, carrying the
sweet scent of wood smoke through the house.

In just a minute she'd find the energy to—

Shadows danced in an odd pattern across the walnut bookshelves at the far side of the room.

Emily blinked. She must be more exhausted than she
had realized. For a moment she had actually thought
someone was standing in the corner watching her. A
man.

A draft of cold air blew across the room, like an icy
hand palming the back of her neck. She shivered and
pulled an afghan around her shoulders. The cozy fire
wasn't making it in the big, high-ceilinged room. Winter was going to be downright frigid if she didn't get the
windows recalked.

"Good evening."

Her insides went absolutely still. Her blood stopped flowing. Even her heart skipped a beat.

The sound she'd heard was not the creak of an old house.

Unless her ears had deceived her, she'd just heard a voice. Very deep and totally masculine. Here in her living room.

Panic drove her to her feet. She whirled around.

The shadow stepped away from the bookcase. Big. Tall. And wearing a—

Good lord! She must be dreaming. The man was wearing the frayed uniform of a British redcoat, black hat with military cockade, crimson waist sash and sword included.

"Wh—" The word couldn't get past the lump in her throat. She tried again. "Wh—who are you? And what are you doing in my house?"

In an elegant gesture, the stranger swept off his felt hat and bowed. "Captain Calvert T. Witherspoon, at your service, madam."

Emily pinched herself just to make sure she was awake.

This guy had to be some kind of a nut case to be dressed like that. Maybe a vet who'd lost track of which war he'd fought? Since he didn't seem to be threatening her at the moment, except for the sword strapped to his waist, she concluded her best bet was to brazen her way through this ridiculous scene. Maybe the men in the white coats would show up soon and haul this fruitcake away.

"Captain, I believe you've made a mistake. If you're looking for your men, they've moved on." About two hundred years ago.

"I fear it is you, Mrs. Morrell, who has erred."

The stranger knowing her name was not a good sign. "Look, Worthington—"

"Witherspoon, madam, a proud English surname."

"I'm sure that's true. It's just that you are trespassing in my house—"

"Nay. You are the interloper here."

She planted her fists on her hips. "Now look, buster, I'm about to lose my patience with you. I don't give a fig about your name. What I want is you out of my house in the next two minutes or I'm going to call the police." Between the dim firelight and his dark, shaggy beard, she couldn't read just how dangerous this man might be. She did know he cut an impressive figure, so big he managed to dwarf everything else in the room. Emily included. And she'd never been considered petite.

A prickle of sweat edged down between her breasts. She had the uncomfortable feeling she was about to test what she and Peter had learned in karate class.

Instead of leaving, as she had hoped, the captain sat down in a wing chair as if he owned the place, and stretched out his long legs. Looking too big for the delicate piece of furniture, he casually hooked one booted foot over the other. "You should be asking yourself, dear lady, how I have arrived here in your parlour."

A log broke with a whoosh, sending sparks up the chimney.

"I left the front door unlocked?" she suggested, eyeing him with a mix of surprise and anxiety.

"Unnecessary, I assure you." He looked so smug she wanted to scream. "I merely walked through the wall."

Oh, sure. The guy was a complete loony tune, she decided. Forget he had a sonorous baritone voice that managed to vibrate up and down Emily's spine in a very disquieting way.

"Then I would appreciate it, Mr. Weathermack, if you would please toddle on out the same way you came in."

"It's Witherspoon," he grimaced. "However, if having me walk through a wall is what you would like..." He gave a low chuckle and cocked one raven eyebrow. "Your every wish is my command, madam."

He stood, placed his hat firmly on his head and bowed once again. In three steps he had vanished—into the bookcase!

Emily gasped. Any minute now she was going to wake up from this crazy dream. Clearly, she'd been working way too hard.

A puff of smoke from the fireplace curled out into the room.

"Does that satisfy you?" the stranger's deep voice asked.

She whirled toward the sound. The British captain stood on the far side of the room, an arrogant smile breaking the dark mat of his beard.

"How did you—" She shook her head. "A magician. Of course! I've seen David Copperfield perform exactly that same trick. Special effects and all. I've never understood how—"

"I am *not* a magician!" Calvert bellowed. "I am a *ghost!*"

She threw up her arms in dismay. "That's it, fella. You're out of here. Any way you want—through the door or out the window, it doesn't matter to me." She pointed to the exit. "Get out. Now. And don't you dare bang that sword against the wood paneling in the hallway. You hear me?"

"Ah, madam, you are a hard woman to convince."

When he drew his sword from its sheath, Emily retreated several steps. She wrapped her hand around an ornate and very heavy bookend. "Stay back," she warned.

"For days I have been trying to convince you this house is inhabited by a ghost. You simply will not believe me. I've tried chains, moans, groans and ridiculous bed sheets to no avail." He sounded almost as weary as she.

"You're the one who's been making all that racket?" What an absurd idea.

"Now I shall demonstrate that, in spite of what you see or believe, I have no substance." He held the sword at arm's length, tilted the tip and ran it through his stomach. He turned so she could see the blade jutting out his back, firelight catching the shiny metal in diamond stars.

Nausea threatened. She edged toward the door, the bookend still firmly in her hand. "You really should go on television, Captain Woodenspoon. You'd be a real hit." She forced a calmness into her voice she didn't feel. "I'd be happy to give you a recommendation, if you'd like." Her heart thudded against her ribs. A few more steps and she'd be—

"Are you dense, madam? I am—"

She bolted. Running, she whizzed out the living room door, down the hall, into the kitchen, yanked the phone off the hook and sank down out of sight behind the counter. She dialed 911. Her breath came in quick little gasps.

"I've got a prowler in the house. Come quick. *Please*. He's crazy." And big and very intimidating.

Never in her entire life had Emily cowered. Until now. Indeed, until this moment she'd had no reason to be terrified of more than a wayward spider.

She trembled. Her stomach churned. She prayed. Lord, did she pray. *Please don't let him hurt my children*. And she listened for approaching sirens. Or the sound of footsteps.

"They won't be able to find me, you know."

Her head snapped up. He stood above her, towered above her. His eyes were blue and mocking, and strangely compelling. She wanted to speak but couldn't find her voice.

"I'll simply vanish," he continued. "That's what ghosts do."

Wonderful. Could I help you on your way? Don't forget your sword.

Her heart lurched with relief at the sound of a knock on the front door. She sagged against the wall. Her eyes closed for just an instant, and when she looked again he was gone.

She had the dizzying feeling her whole world had just turned upside down.

"ARE YOU TRYING to tell me, Sheriff Belinger—you, a trained law enforcement officer—that what I saw to-night was a ghost?" Incredulous, Emily finger-combed her hair and tucked the straying strands behind her ears. Her hand shook.

"Well, now, when ya put it just that way, ma'am..." He smoothed the brim of his hat with his jacketed forearm, looking more and more uncomfortable by the minute. "Officially, I couldn't quite say."

She felt a draft scoot across the paneled entryway and shoved the front door fully closed. "Officer, I want this house searched, top to bottom. I assure you I am not some hysterical woman who sees visions of strange men in my house. I was not having a dream. Nor do I believe in ghosts."

"There has been talk—"

"Of ghosts. And we're going to put those tales to rest right now. Among other things, all that nonsense frightens my children, and I won't have it a minute longer. You're going to find that man and haul him off to jail for trespassing. I'll be more than happy to sign a complaint. He's wearing—"

"The uniform of a redcoat. Yes, ma'am, I know."

"Then he will certainly be easy to identify, for a man of your experience," she cajoled. She gestured toward the rest of the house. "Please feel free to look any-where you'd like."

"If that's what you want, ma'am, but it won't do much good."

Emily blew out a frustrated breath. She'd never met so many superstitious people in her entire life. For a moment she longed for the orderliness of logic diagrams and flow charts, then set aside the thought. She was going to make Honorville her home. Somehow she'd manage to deal with these people on a rational basis.

INVISIBLE, CALVERT SAT at the top of the stairs, enjoying the interplay between Emily Morrell and the sheriff. The lady had spunk. He'd give her that. She'd lasted longer in his haunted house than most of her predecessors. Then again, perhaps after all this time he was losing his touch, he considered, a frown tightening his forehead.

After all, he'd never before tiptoed around trying not to wake the *entire* household when he rattled his chains, like he'd avoided disturbing her children since the first night. Cute little mites.

And never once in two hundred years had he silently slipped into a bedchamber to observe a lady in repose.

Emily, he discovered, slept in a sheer gown that would have brought a blush to the cheeks of the most experienced dancing girl. Her mouth was slightly open, inviting, and she hugged a pillow in her sleep. The covers managed to slide down around her waist, and he'd had a most unfamiliar urge to lie down beside her on that big four-poster bed.

He would take her pliable body in his arms, awakening her slowly with soft caresses and quiet kisses at that sensitive spot beneath her ear. No doubt she would moan a little before she fully awakened to his ministrations. Then she would turn in his arms, her eyes at first filled with surprise, which would soon be followed by a good deal of pleasure.

Ah, yes, he had wanted to join her in that comfortable bed.

Not that anything would have resulted from such peculiar behavior. Ghosts, as everyone knew, did not have the same needs as human males. More's the pity....

EMILY LINGERED by the mailbox at the end of the driveway, waiting for the school bus. Pete's first day at school was sure to have been stressful, particularly after the sheriff had spent half the night futilely searching the house and disrupting the children's sleep.

She wanted to be there when Pete got home.

Inhaling deeply of the crisp autumn air, she eased her own feelings of stress by simply enjoying her surroundings. Across the road, the neighbor's sparkling white house was barely visible through a painter's palette of vivid foliage. A postcard-perfect covered bridge, gray with age, provided the entrance to their long drive that wove through the trees. High above her, wild geese honked their departure for points south and arrowed across a cloudless sky.

The neighbor's white horse trotted toward the rock wall across the road. As he neared and spotted Emily, he shied, reared and galloped back the way he had come, his hoofbeats crashing through the woods.

"Gracious, I'll have to bring you an apple from my yard so you won't be afraid of me," she whispered, chuckling to herself. She'd never thought of herself as so frightening she'd scare off an animal.

Still smiling, she glanced behind her to see if Becky had decided to join her. Framed as it was by two striking maples, the house looked exceptionally welcoming, with the carriage house just visible off to the side. Someday she'd make that into a family suite for guests, but for now it served for extra storage and as her garage.

Turning back, she heard the sound of gears shifting and the grind of the old bus slowly making its way up the hill on the road that led past Henderson House.

Stuffing the day's junk mail in the hip pocket of her jeans, Emily watched the yellow bus draw to a stop in front of her. The aging driver gave her a single nod while Pete clambered down the steps. As the bus pulled away, leaving a trail of diesel fumes, she could see her son's shoulders hunched and his footsteps dragging. This had not been a good day for the nine-year-old, and her heart twisted for the adjustments he would have to make in his new home.

Forcing aside the doubts that suddenly assailed her, she gave him a quick hug. His hair smelled of little boy sweat and his shirttail hung out of his pants.

"Hard day?" she asked sympathetically.

"Okay, I guess." His voice flat, he shrugged. "They said I talk funny."

"I suppose we do sound different than they do. It's our accents." Or lack of them, she thought. Some of the locals she could barely understand.

He pulled away. "Can I have somethin' to eat?"

"Sure, honey. Becky and I made cookies this morning. She's got a plate all ready for you. Milk's in the fridge."

He headed up the driveway with halfhearted enthusiasm, his feet shuffling through the leaves at the edge of the path. Before Emily could follow, she heard a deep and disturbingly familiar voice behind her.

"It's always hard to be the new boy in school."

Her heart sank to somewhere in the vicinity of her stomach, and she felt a sudden surge of adrenaline through her veins. She fought off an urge to race up the driveway to the house and lock the door behind her.

Turning, she found the British captain sitting plain as you please on the rock fence. Two minutes ago she'd been standing beside the road all alone. The guy had the darnedest way of popping up out of nowhere. But not for a moment would she let him know he'd startled her.

"What are you doing here?" she asked impatiently.

"I've been waiting with you for Peter to come home."

"Hiding in the shrubbery, I suppose." And frightening the neighbor's horse, she realized.

"Not at all, my dear." He tipped his hat to the back of his head, letting a lock of dark hair fall rakishly across his forehead. "When I choose, no one can see me. Not even you."

But the horse did. "Perhaps I didn't make myself entirely clear last night. I do not *wish* to see you anywhere near my house. The sheriff—"

"—is an incompetent toad."

She slanted him her most stern look. In the daylight he looked less intimidating than he had in the shadows of her living room. This time he wasn't wearing his sword, and his tunic collar was open, revealing a tempting brush of midnight-black hair. He looked thoroughly relaxed. Emily wished she could say the same for herself. Something about this man really had her on edge, and it wasn't entirely because of the way he appeared so unexpectedly. He was young, she realized, perhaps in his thirties, without a trace of gray in his beard.

And devilishly attractive.

"Why don't you just go on home, Captain—"

"Witherspoon," he added before she could make a hash of his name again. "Alas, my home is in Essex. A long way, I fear, and I have vowed not to return to my homeland until I have proven my innocence."

"Innocence?" Her voice cracked. Lord, was she dealing with a mass murderer?

He slid off the rock wall and brushed the dirt from his hands. "Of betraying my country."

"You're a traitor to England?" A better choice than being Blackbeard, whom he closely resembled.

"Never!" he bellowed. "I was falsely accused. Foolishly led astray by a comely wench, I admit, but never a traitor!"

His adamant denial of guilt rang with a fair amount of truth, Emily decided, surprised by the tug of sympathy she felt for this strange, dark, unkempt man. "Perhaps if you talked to Traveler's Aid they'd find a way to get you home again." Or into a mental hospital where you could get some help.

"You don't believe me, do you?" He eyed her skeptically.

"I believe you're not a traitor."

As though a weight had been lifted, he straightened his shoulders, and the roughness of his whiskered features softened. "In more than two hundred years, you are the first, dear lady, to have said those kind words. You have my undying gratitude." His head dipped in a regal gesture of acknowledgment.

"Well, yes..." she stammered. The poor man looked like he might cry. Whatever was she supposed to do now? "You'll have to excuse me. I want to hear about Pete's day at school." She smiled weakly and turned to walk to the house.

He fell into step beside her. "This town is not very friendly to strangers," he observed.

"Friendship takes time. They'll get used to us." Odd, she thought. Her tennis shoes made crunching noises on the gravel as she walked, but the captain's boots didn't seem to make any sound at all. "We've only been here a few days."

"And no one has yet called to welcome you."

"True. They're probably waiting to give us a little more time to settle in." Although, at the hardware store that morning, every customer had turned silent when she entered, almost as though the townspeople felt an animosity toward her. Added to the unpleasant reception Mrs. Pierce had given her at the drug store a few days ago, it had given her the creeps. Emily had expected New England caution on the part of her new neighbors, but not an undercurrent of anger.

The captain's voice drew Emily back to the present.

She slanted a glance at the man walking beside her. In his odd way, the captain was the most pleasant person she'd met so far. Also the best looking—in spite of his unusual clothing and his dark beard. He had thick, expressive eyebrows and long, black lashes that any woman would envy. His eyes were alight with intelligence and underlying humor. More than once those eyes had mocked her—and made her feel very much like a woman. She wasn't at all sure that reaction was a good idea.

She even liked the way he spoke in a sonorous, accented voice rather like an antiquated BBC commentator.

"Your son is likely to suffer at school," he said. "I remember as a young lad being taunted by the older boys." He walked with his hands clasped behind his back. "It was a most unpleasant experience."

His obvious concern for her son surprised Emily. "Pete's very outgoing. I'm sure he'll make friends quickly." Although it didn't look like his first day at school had been a success.

They'd reached the porch, a wide expanse with white columns marking the distance every few feet across the width of house. The stranger seemed quite set on going on up the steps with her.

"Captain Witherspoon..." she began, then corrected herself in the hope of gaining his cooperation. "Calvert, if you're homeless, I'm sure Honorville has some sort of social service agency that could find you a place to stay."

He glanced up at the dormer window above the porch and smiled benignly. "That's most kind of you, madam, but I assure you, my quarters are quite comfortable."

Emily cocked her head suspiciously. What did this guy have on his mind? She wasn't at all ready to take on roomers, regardless of how physically attractive this one might be. As far as she was concerned, he was downright dangerous.

The screen door creaked open. Pete appeared, glass in one hand, cookie in the other, and a mustache of milk above his upper lip.

"Mom, the teacher says I gotta write a report on George Washington. Can you help me?"

"Of course, dear. I'll be right in." She turned to send Calvert on his way, but he wasn't there. All she heard was the echo of a muttered curse.

The muscles of her stomach tightened. "Pete, the man I was talking to. Did you see where he went?"

"I didn't see anybody."

"But he was right there," she insisted numbly, following her son into the house. Men didn't just vanish—or appear out of the blue. There had to be some reasonable explanation for Calvert Witherspoon, she assured herself.

As soon as she got Pete working on his report, Emily wandered upstairs, making a point of setting aside a bad case of jitters that threatened. There was really no cause, she assured herself.

She peered into the bedrooms, each furnished with original eighteenth-century pieces that an antique dealer would die for. Henderson House was quite an inheritance, she thought, congratulating herself once more on her plan to turn it into a B and B. With a few repairs and a couple of new bathrooms, the place was ideal. Fortunately, some prior occupant had added electricity and a decent furnace.

Though she searched everywhere, the only thing she found out of the ordinary was a Queen Anne chair that seemed to be rocking on its own, pushed by a draft from the open window, she supposed. Certainly there was no bearded man lurking in her house, she thought as she firmly locked the front door.

After the children were bathed and tucked in for the night, Emily settled down at her computer. She pulled the expense file onto the screen and began bringing the data up to date. No sooner had she started than the figures began to swim in front of her eyes. The rows and columns actually shimmered and waved.

She blinked and rubbed at the bridge of her nose. Maybe she needed glasses.

When she looked at the screen again he was there. On a monochrome monitor, Calvert T. Witherspoon's face smiled back at her in living color.

"Darn it all! Quit bugging me!"

Assuming that what she saw was his reflection, she turned around to glare at the impossible man. Why couldn't he simply leave her alone?

There was no one there. Her office, with its heaps of unpacked boxes, was empty.

But his face was still on the screen. Smirking.

She yanked a tissue from a box and tried to wipe him away. Now that was a foolish reaction, she admitted.

"What do you call this device?" he asked, looking from side to side as though he was checking out the circuits.

"It's a computer. *My* computer." He had to be using mirrors. Secret passageways through the house. Peepholes in the ceiling. She'd figure out his silly game and then throw him out on his ear.

"Did you know when you. . ." He waved his fingers in the air. "What do you call what you were doing?"

"I was typing in my expense reports. Do you mind?"

"Well, when you type it actually tickles. Quite an extraordinary experience being inside this box."

"You are *not* in my computer, Calvert! Come out here where I can—"

"My dear Emily, you are the most stubborn woman I have ever had the misfortune to meet. I will simply have to prove once again you are wrong."

The red light fluttered wildly on her hard disk. Symbols—hearts, spades and other oddities—danced pell-mell across the screen. The motor roared. She envisioned metal scraping upon metal.

"Cal! Stop what you're doing. My God, you're going to crash my hard disk!" Fatigue, frustration and fear made her sob. "It'll take me hours to—" The screen went dark and his face reappeared.

"I do not believe I have done any serious damage," he said, his voice almost like a velvet caress, "and I regret I had to frighten you. But you must now see that you cannot stay in this house. You have already shown great courage by remaining as long as you have. Go back—to wherever you came from." His blue eyes gazed at her in near desperation.

She leaned her elbows on the tabletop and rested her chin in her hands. "Look, Cal, let me explain." Having a rational conversation with a man who thought he was a ghost seemed impossible. Yet what else could she do but remain calm and hope for the best? "I sold my home in California. With that money I'm going to restore Henderson House to its former beauty. The workmen will be starting tomorrow on the outside—the roof and siding, primarily. During the winter I'll fix up the inside of the house. Come spring I'll be renting out rooms, because by then I will be broke."

"You actually expect people to stay in a haunted house?" he asked incredulously. "Why, I'd frighten them out of their wits."

"You'll do no such thing." In fact, her concept for a marketing brochure included a reference to the tale of the Henderson ghost. She figured that little trick would be a big draw for the curious.

"You must leave, Emily."

Her jaw tightened. No would-be ghost was going to drive her out of her home. "I'm not going anywhere, Cal. You can just get used to that idea right now."

A sigh that seemed to come up from deep in his soul shimmered the screen. "As much as I find you very pleasant company, Emily, I cannot allow you to stay."

"Too bad, Cal. I tried to be reasonable with you. My leaving is not one of the choices."

Reaching to the side of the computer, she switched it off. As the screen went dark, she heard a strangled groan.

Gotcha!

Chapter Three

Impertinent. Willful. Obstinate. Intractable.

With each pacing step across his room, Calvert discovered another word to describe Emily Morrell.

She'd been here a week, by damn, and hadn't budged one single inch. He'd tried every trick he could think of. At one point she'd actually snatched a bed sheet right out of his hand, blaming herself for knocking a freshly washed sheet off the top stair railing. Nothing, absolutely nothing, could convince her that Calvert T. Witherspoon was a ghost, much less run her out of the house. Even now there were workmen scampering all over the roof, making such a din with their hammers and saws he could barely hear himself think.

Finally, Calvert paused by the window. She was down there talking to one of the carpenters, her head held at that haughty, stubborn angle he'd grown to expect. The soft wool sweater she wore was the kind a man ached to touch, and her tight trousers outlined her shape in exquisite detail. Nicely rounded bottom, well-formed legs, and the sweater clung in exactly the right places.

A smile tugged at the corners of his lips. Beginning deep in his gut, a laugh began. A roaring, invigorating, felt-good-clear-down-to-his-toes kind of laugh he hadn't felt in years.

He threw up his arms at the sheer joy of the experience.

"By thunder! She is the most magnificent creature I have ever met."

Like a master chess player, she had outmaneuvered him at every opportunity. She had even managed to get the children on her side, ignoring his efforts to disturb the household, as though he did not exist. An incredible feat, given his vast array of talents.

If she had been a general in the rebellion, the colonists would have won the war in half the time. Not that he was prepared to surrender, of course. But he was certainly running out of gunpowder and shot.

His laugh caught in his throat when, from the corner of his eye, he saw the bedroom door swing open.

Becky stood in the doorway gawking at him, her eyes wide and innocent, just as clear a blue as Emily's and equally beguiling. A doll dangled from her hand.

"Hi, mister. You wanna play?"

She could see him? He scratched at his beard. Maybe it was because she was so young that he was visible to Becky. Or perhaps she'd simply caught him off guard. To vanish now would frighten the child. For some inexplicable reason he didn't want to do that.

"Mommy said I was s'posed to stay out of the way of the work's men. Are you a work's men?"

"No, I don't think so."

"Then will you play with me?"

He cleared his throat. "I'm not quite sure I know how to play with little girls."

Her smile brightened like sunbeams dancing across a still pond, and Calvert's heart constricted. Good Lord, how he remembered playing with his younger sisters, teasing them and loving the adoration in their eyes. Those were glorious days, those years before his father had decided he was a pale imitation of his older brother, not worthy of the Witherspoon name.

"I'll teach you how," Becky insisted. "We can play teatime. My mommy says that's a good game to play with grown-ups."

"You're serving English tea, I trust," he suggested dryly, fighting off a raft of images from the past.

She frowned.

Noting her confusion, he smiled to reassure her and spoke softly. "It does not matter, Becky. I am confident whatever tea you serve will be delicious."

"It's just pretend tea."

"Excellent. My favorite." Perfect for a ghost.

Her little feet took her racing down the hallway and back again within minutes. She clutched a box filled with tiny cups and saucers, and three additional dolls joined the party.

It took a bit of time to change a footlocker into a low tea table, and then they settled down, the dolls, Becky—and Calvert, sitting awkwardly on the floor with his legs crossed Indian fashion. The child carefully poured invisible liquid into each cup.

He took the first sip. "Magnificent. I had forgotten how refreshing a good spot of English tea could be."

She giggled and pretended to drink from her cup with a noisy slurp.

"Now, now," he admonished, "a lady drinks silently. Very quietly. Like this." Lifting his cup, he curled his baby finger just so, and pressed the rim to his lips. "Then you must smile at your partner and nod. Nodding is quite an art in England, you know. Quite sophisticated. It takes English women years to get it just right."

Mimicking his instructions, she drank again as though she were having tea with the queen.

"How come you don't have to comb your hair?" she asked as she helped each of her dolls to some tea.

"It has hardly seemed necessary of late." Not for the last couple of centuries.

"Mommy says I gots to comb my hair every day, and brush it, too, so's it gets shiny. My mommy's hair is real soft."

"Is it now." He'd suspected as much. Indeed, as he thought about it, he recalled how even a light breeze could tug at Emily's curls, shifting them about her face in an ever-changing pattern until she was forced to tame them with her hand. Lovely.

"Mommy would brush your hair, if you wants. She's real good and doesn't yank the knots too hard."

"I appreciate your offer, Becky, but I'm not at all sure your mother would be pleased with the idea."

Amazingly, the prospect of Emily combing his hair had a rather great appeal. He imagined her standing close to him, imagined catching her scent, feeling the warmth of her body as she accidently brushed against his shoulder. Her breath would be as sweet as rose petals, her hands as gentle as a spring breeze.

He had watched the family as they dined each evening, drawn by their laughter and a futile hope of seeing Emily dressed in a formal gown that would display her endowments to his satisfaction—the creamy swell of her breasts, which he longed to touch, to kiss, to hold within his palms.

An uncomfortable, and thoroughly unforgettable, ache formed between his thighs. A pox on such nonsense! He was a *ghost!*

Clearing his throat, he said, "Becky, while this interlude has been most pleasant, I believe we must end our teatime."

By all that was holy, he should not be having such thoughts about Emily Morrell. Instead, he should be concentrating on his search for the diary that would clear his name of traitorous slander. A search that had been entirely futile for two hundred years.

EMILY WAS NEARLY at her wit's end. The entire crew of workmen was threatening to quit.

"Mr. Middleberry, you're the foreman. I hired you to get the job done." She watched as two of the crew gathered up their tools—remaining tools, she mentally corrected—and climbed into the back of a pickup truck. Middleberry was the only man in Honorville who resembled a contractor. She'd intentionally selected a local person, hoping that would please the townspeople. "Surely you can convince the men to stay."

"There's been odd things goin' on, missus. Tools gone missin'. Ladders moved to where they weren't. It makes the boys a bit skittery, that 'n' the stories 'boot the ghost."

"Really, Mr. Middleberry, I'm sure there's a logical explanation for everything." She suspected it might well have something to do with the loony tune she'd inherited along with the house. If she could keep the men on the job, she'd see to Captain Witherspoon herself. "The men probably just put down their tools and forgot them. As for the ladders—"

"Sorry, missus." He placed his cap back on his balding head. "We all decided together, like. Nothin' but trouble comes from working for a Henderson, they says. Got us another job over to Waverton that will keep us workin' a spell."

"But you agreed—" It was no use. No matter that Emily's name was Morrell, not Henderson. The foreman and his men were going to leave her with a half-finished roof and the paint still chipping off the siding. They'd left her in the worst possible predicament.

She glared up at the windows above the porch and balled her hands into fists. *Damn him!* What gave him the right to jeopardize all of her plans?

Becky burst out through the front door, hopping and skipping down the steps.

"Hi, Mommy. I found a new friend."

"Not now, honey, I've got something I have to do." She was in no mood to deal with another of Becky's imaginary playmates.

"He's a big, tall man with a funny whiskers."

A band tightened around Emily's chest. She knelt down beside her daughter. "Where were you playing with the man?"

"Upstairs." She pointed to the window above the porch. "We played teatime. He says English ladies drink tea *veeery* quietly. What's an English lady, Mommy?"

"I'll tell you later. Did anything else happen, honey?"

"Nuh-uh. My dollies and me drinked up all the pretend tea. Then he said it was time to go. He was a nice man."

"I hope so." Children were usually good judges of character. Emily sincerely hoped her daughter was right in this case. "Becky, you wait here on the porch for Pete to come home. Don't go wandering off. He'll be here soon. I'm going to go upstairs and talk to the nice man."

Her heart pounding extra-hard, Emily made her way up the stairs to the attic. She shoved open the door.

A narrow bed with an oak headboard sat at one side of the room, an old quilt strewn carelessly over the mattress. A footlocker had been shoved into the middle of the room next to the Queen Anne rocker. The locker looked far too heavy for Becky to have moved by herself, yet it was easy to envision her little cups and saucers arrayed there for a game of pretend tea. Opposite the bed there was a matching oak dresser, and on it, Captain Witherspoon's hat.

"Cal," she called softly. "I know you're here somewhere. Please come out from wherever you hide yourself. We need to talk."

He appeared. Right in the middle of the room. He hadn't walked through a wall. Or come through some secret passageway. He was simply there.

Emily swallowed hard. "You've been playing with my daughter."

"A charming child. Brews an excellent pot of tea. The best I've had in some years."

"You didn't... You wouldn't..."

Shifting his stance, Calvert puzzled over Emily's hesitancy, the high flush on her cheeks, the tension in the way she held herself. It took a moment for him to realize the problem.

"Oh, my dear Emily," he said with a sigh. "That you would think I might harm Becky cuts me to the quick. Truly it does. She is as bright as a diamond and reminds me very much of my sisters."

"You have sisters?"

"Aye. Abigail and Victoria. Little mischief makers they were. As was I," he conceded with a reminiscing chuckle. He wanted to reassure Emily that he would never hurt her daughter. "You see, we had this marvelous tower room in the old family castle. I suppose they'd once locked prisoners inside, but it was our favorite place, cold and drafty though it was. During winter we'd make dozens of snowballs and secretly haul buckets of them to the tower room. Then, when a visitor arrived..."

A smile tugged at the corners of Emily's lovely, rosy lips and she visibly relaxed.

"Ah, how well I remember the day the dowager Lady Claudia came to call," he continued. If he could only just take Emily's hands in his, she would know she had nothing to fear for her daughter. "Dreadful woman. Quite dour, I assure you. Always pinching my sisters' cheeks and forcing me to behave myself in a most gentlemanly manner. I'm afraid we laid on a rather heavy barrage of snowballs that day. Nearly drowned the poor ol' thing wrapped up as she was right there in her open carriage. I doubt she was ever quite the same again."

Emily's soft laughter wrapped itself around Calvert like a warm winter blanket. He had the urge to pull her into his arms and more fully experience the sensation of her nearness. But, of course, that was not possible.

"I imagine your parents were not amused?" she asked, her eyes now alight with the humor of his story.

Thoughtfully, he raised one eyebrow. "I think perhaps my mother was. Lady Claudia was not her favorite person. Though she never would have said so. My father, you see, was quite stern and her ladyship was some distant relative of his, I believe."

Emily pressed her lips together. How very odd to be talking to this strange man about a past that included castle towers, and actually believing his story. At some deep, intuitive level, she did believe him, though for the life of her, she didn't know why. It wasn't at all logical.

She was also absolutely confident Calvert would never hurt Becky. For that she was incredibly grateful—but it didn't solve her other problems.

"Cal, nothing about you makes any sense to me. You appear out of nowhere, and I don't know why."

"I have explained—"

"At this point it doesn't really matter. I have a problem that I can't solve without your cooperation." She waited for him to speak, but he remained silent. "I assume you were responsible for the workmen misplacing their tools and for the ladders hopping about on their own."

"I haven't had any success frightening you off with my usual repertory of tricks, so I tried the next best strategy. I believe it is called a flanking maneuver." He clasped his hands behind his back. "Rather cleverly done, if I do say so myself."

"So clever they've all left."

"I find the silence quite gratifying."

"I don't!" she said with conviction. "I've got a roof that's going to leak like a sieve the next time it rains and not a single hope of getting it fixed . . . except you."

He pulled back in surprise. "Me? Why, I know nothing about repairing roofs. You will simply have to give up your idea of occupying this house—"

"Not on your life. I'm hiring you, Cal. You and I are going to finish the roof and then we'll start painting the siding. I'll pay you a reasonable wage plus room and board. With any luck we should be able to get most of the work done before it snows. Whatever painting we can't finish will just have to wait until Spring."

Emily's announcement rocked Calvert back on his heels. The audacity of the woman! She wanted him to work as a simple hireling? For wages? A pittance, no doubt. Plus a few scraps of bread. A ridiculous notion.

And he loved the idea! He'd been dreadfully bored for the last hundred years. What better pick-me-up than a little hard work. Sets a man's head on the right track again, or so he'd been told.

Suppressing a smile, he nodded in his most British fashion. "Very well, madam, you have a new carpenter."

"Good. I'm glad we have that settled." She extended her hand to bind the agreement.

Calvert's training ran deep. A handshake offered in good faith could not be ignored. Honor required he respond in kind.

Her small hand almost vanished within his larger one. Her fingers were long, the bones delicate ridges he caressed with his thumb, yet her grip was amazingly strong. And warm. Calvert hadn't touched another human in more than two hundred years. In a way he couldn't quite fathom, he felt he had simply been marking time waiting for Emily Morrell to appear at Henderson House. He wanted to go on holding her hand for another century or so.

"Dinner will be ready about six," she said, slipping from his grasp, the color in her cheeks high again, as though she had experienced something far more than a simple business agreement.

"That really isn't necessary. I haven't eaten in years."

"Then you should have a good appetite by supper time." She turned to leave, then looked back over her shoulder. "Because of the children, would you please wash up a bit? Comb your hair? You wouldn't want to set a bad example."

"Of course not, dear lady. I shall be the epitome of proper decorum."

"And one more favor?"

He raised a questioning eyebrow.

"Don't tell the children you're a ghost. It would just confuse them."

"As you wish, my dear." Smiling, he bowed as she hurried out the door.

IN SPITE OF HERSELF, Emily had to admit Cal was a devastating figure of a man. He'd trimmed his hair, and it was a lustrous black with soft waves that just brushed the top of his collar; his neatly shaped beard gave him an arrogant air. Somehow he'd managed to remove the worst of the oily spots on his tunic. As one of her young single friends might say, "This guy cleans up *real* good."

Taking a break from regaling her children with stories of his youth, Cal looked across the cherrywood dining table and caught her eye. For a moment, he studied her, his fork poised in midair, then his gaze lifted to her hair, sweeping her with a caress she could almost feel. His eyes narrowed. Lazily, his perusal wandered across her face again, sliding down her neck to breasts that had suddenly warmed with an undeniable heaviness.

Like an embarrassed adolescent, Emily lowered her gaze to her plate. Lord, she hadn't been *interested* in a man since Ted died. Oh, she'd had a few dates and certainly didn't expect to remain celibate the rest of her life. At least, she hoped that wouldn't be the case.

But this guy was a mental case. He had to be. Nobody who had his act together thought of himself as a ghost.

Yet she reacted to him at some basic, primal level that had her head spinning. *Interested* was decidedly an understatement and not in the least logical. Her palms were damp; she could hardly catch her breath. Her appetite had fled. All the while, Cal was managing to devour his third helping of pot roast while conversing casually with her children as though nothing was amiss.

And before dinner, when he'd briefly held her hand, she'd had the oddest feeling of . . . coming home.

There'd been other feelings, too, ones she wasn't entirely willing to acknowledge. And images. Flashes of her and Cal doing intimate things together that had brought a rush of heat to her cheeks.

Goodness, she hadn't blushed in years. Nor had she indulged in such erotic thoughts.

Definitely an experience she hadn't expected where Captain Witherspoon was concerned.

Worst of all, she realized how much she'd missed the sound of a man's voice at the dinner table—and how much her children needed a masculine presence. Calvert T. Witherspoon was definitely all male. Broad shoulders. Narrow waist accented by his tailored tunic. And sky-blue eyes that gleamed with wicked laughter at the least little joke.

Self-consciously, her hand went to her throat and she fingered the plain gold necklace she wore. Somehow she was going to have to rein in her wayward thoughts.

Maybe she needed to find a local doctor and get a checkup. She hadn't felt quite right since her move from California. Or rather, since Cal had entered her life.

Calvert levered his fork and savored another bite of tender beef, his gaze following Emily's gesture to that inviting spot at the base of her throat. With an effort, he forced himself to consider the food on his plate, not other delicious tastes that would not be his to enjoy.

He'd always assumed a ghost didn't need to eat. In fact, probably couldn't eat. And here he was enjoying a fine meal after all these years.

Quite amazing.

Enjoying the company, too, he admitted. Becky and Pete were bright little tykes, but it was Emily who had him thoroughly unnerved. Sitting at the head of the table, she'd created a warm family scene and had drawn him into the picture. The lights from the chandelier highlighted her silken hair and cast soft shadows across her face. Honey-colored lashes fanned her cheeks. The sound of her melodious laughter settled in his chest, curling into a spot that had been empty for a long, long time.

In another time, another place, he would be quite content to pursue the lady—and seduce her with all the experience and skill that had once been his hallmark.

Images came to him of carrying Emily up the stairs to her bedroom, placing her gently on that big four-poster and joining her there where he could explore all of her delectable curves. He saw himself stroking her, caressing her warm, pliable flesh, tasting the sweetness of her lips, discovering for himself just how soft and fragrant her hair might be.

Tarnation! Ghosts did not *do* that.

Whatever would Emily think if she could read his mind? She might not believe he was a ghost, but his thoughts would scare her far more than any clanking chain had managed to do. He didn't want that.

With an effort, he dragged his gaze from Emily and studied young Peter sitting next to him.

"Looks like you've gotten yourself a bruise, lad," he observed.

The boy rubbed his jaw. "It's nuthin'."

"Peter, have you been in a fight?" Emily asked, frowning. "Why didn't you tell me?"

"Just some guys, Mom."

"Guys?"

"A couple." Pete studiously continued with his meal.

"You know I don't believe in fighting," his mother admonished.

"Sometimes a lad finds himself in a situation he simply cannot avoid," Calvert suggested. He'd found himself in that sort of spot more than once. "Did you fight back, lad?"

"He's had karate lessons," his mother inserted.

Calvert flicked Emily a silencing glance which she totally ignored. Surely she realized this was man's work.

"That doesn't help, Mom, if some guy has you by the arms and he's twice your size and he's got some friend who's lettin' you have it."

Angry, red spots appeared on Emily's fair cheeks. "The bullies! What are their names? I'll just go to school next week and have a chat with the principal. That sort of thing shouldn't—"

"Aw, Mom..."

"If you will permit me to assist." Calvert looped his arm around Peter's shoulders. "I have some small experience in the manly art of self-defense. I would be more than happy to share my knowledge with the boy. For his own protection, you understand."

Emily looked doubtful. "Boxing?"

"Hey, yeah, Mom." The boy's eyes rounded eagerly. "Could Cal teach me? Then I could show those guys—"

"Well . . . only if you understand you can't fight unless someone else starts it first."

The doorbell chimed and Emily was almost relieved, though she couldn't imagine who'd come to call at this hour.

"I'll get it," she announced, dropping her napkin beside her plate. She'd deal with Peter's boxing activities and her own strange feelings about Cal later.

Berating herself for not noticing Peter's bruised jaw earlier, she opened the door to find Brady Berrington standing on her porch. His suit jacket hung from his narrow shoulders as though he had borrowed it from the garden scarecrow.

"Hiya, Emily. Hope I haven't caught you at a bad time."

"Not at all. We were just finishing up dinner." *My family and our resident ghost,* she thought with an internal groan. *How would she ever explain Cal away?* "Come on in." She carefully led Brady into the living room.

"Heard you had a bit of trouble today."

"If having a whole crew walk off the job when it was only half-done is considered trouble, then you heard right." She sat down on the couch and he joined her, his long legs nearly folding double as he sank into the cushion.

"That's a real shame. I suppose you'll have to give up your dream."

"Of turning Henderson House into a B and B?" She shook her head. "Not at all. I see it as only a temporary setback."

"But how will you manage, Emily? You'd have to hire roofers from as far away as Concord. With the travel time and all..." He took her hand. "The expense would be enormous. Surely it would be better to let a new buyer concern himself with such a difficult task."

Slipping away from his grasp, she stood. For some reason this guy gave her the willies, though he'd always been a perfect gentleman—well, almost. She wasn't pleased how he always managed to touch her. "I'll get by, Brady. I've, uh, hired a handyman to help me out."

A frown darkened his features. "Somebody local?"

"I think he's been around for a while." A good long time, if she were to believe Cal's cock-and-bull story.

"I do wish you'd reconsider this whole project. For years my father tried to encourage your great-aunt to sell this old place, but she simply wouldn't listen to reason. After being here for a week, surely you see—"

"I see a wonderful old house that can be both my home and my business." She folded her arms. "I don't discourage easily, Brady, and I'd prefer you didn't bring up the subject of my selling the house again."

With minimal courtesy, Emily escorted him to the door. When she turned around, Cal was standing in the paneled entryway—with his sword!

"What on earth are you doing with that weapon? You'll hurt someone."

"I'm here to protect your honor, my dear. Should the need arise."

She suppressed a smile. Cal the Gallant Ghost? "My honor is fully intact, thank you."

"The man's a rotter if I ever saw one," he said grimly. "Beady eyes, you know. Wouldn't trust him to feed my hounds."

"I'm not exactly fond of him myself. I think he's harmless, though. Just more interested in a commission than anything else." She sighed and stared thoughtfully into the distance. "I don't know quite how I'll explain it, but you realize we have to give the workmen back their tools."

Calvert was struck once again by the marvel of Emily. Nothing, absolutely nothing, was going to get in the way of her dreams.

"SHE'S DETERMINED to stay."

"We can't let that happen."

"That was very clever of you to misplace the roofer's tools."

The sound of a throat being cleared preceded "That wasn't my doing."

"Now don't start that. We've used the Henderson ghost story to our advantage for years. No need to start believing it now."

"She's found someone to help her."

"Who?"

The only response was a shaking of heads.

"Somehow we're going to have to get her to sell—or simply leave."

"How?"

"I don't know, but for the sake of Honorville we'll have to find a way—before she finds the diary."

Chapter Four

Emily clung tightly to each rung as she crept up the ladder. The roof was a dizzying height, farther above the ground than she had realized. Maybe if she didn't look down she'd be all right.

Cal's hammer struck an irregular beat somewhere above her. He'd gone to work right after breakfast while she had cleaned up the dishes and set Becky to the chore of displaying her fancy-dress dolls in an old bookcase in the hallway.

When she got her first full view of the roof backlit by the morning sun, Emily's breath lodged in her throat.

A hammer seemed to be moving through air of its own accord, bashing itself on a shingle—tap, tap, ta-tap. Just the hammer. No arm holding it. No workman. No Cal.

The electrical impulses in Emily's brain did a good imitation of a short circuit. Fighting off the disorientating sensation, she grasped the ladder more tightly.

Logically, what she was seeing, or rather *wasn't* seeing, couldn't be happening. But it was.

"Cal?" His name came out as a croak.

The hammer stopped its drumming beat. It simply hung suspended in midair. "Terrific view from up here," Cal's disembodied voice announced. "You can see all the way to the White Mountains from the top of the roof. Come have a look."

Emily wavered. "Cal, you're...invis—" What total nonsense. "I...can't see you." Maybe she was the one who needed psychiatric care—on an emergency basis.

"Oh. Sorry." He appeared, hammer in hand. Simply there where he hadn't been a moment before. He'd shed his tunic and was bare from the waist up, dark hair furring his broad chest, his legs encased in his tight-fitting uniform breeches.

Closing her eyes and leaning her forehead against the top rung of the ladder, Emily took three deep breaths. The world was sure to stop spinning soon.

"Are you all right, lass?"

She opened her eyes. He stood next to the ladder, his expression filled with concern.

"I guess I'm not real good with heights," she admitted. Or with men who can make themselves invisible. Maybe it was just the odd angle of the sun in her eyes, she thought hopefully. Surely that was the case.

"Here, let me help you."

He steadied her by the arm as she stepped onto the roof. His hand at her elbow felt strong, warm and thoroughly human. Emily regained some small sense of equilibrium.

"You really mustn't do that, you know," she said.

"Do what?"

"Your disappearing act. Taking advantage of optical illusions, I imagine. It's very disconcerting."

He gave her a cocky grin. "I suppose it is."

"And what if someone came up the drive and saw...or rather, didn't see you? What would they think?"

"That something was amiss, I imagine."

"They certainly would," she agreed. Lord, there was nothing insubstantial about Cal now, she noticed. His arms were well muscled, his stomach flat, and he had the kind of chest a woman wanted to touch. Often and intimately.

There ought to be a law against a man like Cal going without a shirt, she thought. Her hands actually itched with the desire to run her fingers through the curling hair on his chest, to palm his well-defined pectorals, and feel his nipples harden to her touch. Standing so close, she caught his masculine scent, a sexy mixture of clean sweat and sawdust. Somewhere low in her body, she felt her muscles go taut, a thoroughly female reaction to the sight and smell of a very virile male.

Dear God! She had to stop thinking like that.

With an effort, she forced her thoughts back to the task at hand. "Shall we get to work?"

He bowed in a courtly manner. "'Tis a hard taskmaster you are, madam."

She took up a position just above where he had laid a row of asphalt shingles and began to lay an overlapping tier. Though the autumn air was cool, a sheen of perspiration soon formed on her face. She shrugged off her Windbreaker and tossed it aside, taking up her hammer once again.

As she worked she was acutely aware of Cal, his agile movements, the way his muscles flexed with each stroke of the hammer, and the smattering of freckles across his broad shoulders. His complexion was more fair than she might have expected from the darkness of his hair, and very appealing. Everything about the man radiated a powerful current of sexuality. Emily reacted as though celibacy was a bad habit she'd like to break. In the next fifteen minutes.

But with a man who thought he was a ghost? And sometimes appeared to be just that? Not a rational idea at all.

She could ask him to wear his tunic while he worked, she thought, deciding she'd be able to concentrate better on her own job if he were fully clothed. But that would appear equally odd to any stranger passing by who happened to see him. Workmen were supposed to wear overalls or jeans, not a two-hundred-year-old British officer's uniform.

"Cal, I think after lunch I'll run into town for a few minutes. Maybe I can pick up a few things for you. A couple of work shirts and some pants?"

"Regretfully, I am without funds at the moment for such a purchase." He hefted a bundle of shingles with ease and placed them where Emily could comfortably reach the stack.

He might not have money but he did have his pride, she realized. She should have thought of that. "We could deduct the cost from your pay, if you'd like. I'd hate for you to ruin your uniform."

"Perhaps that would be a wise course of action."
Standing, he stretched and rubbed at the back of his
neck with his long, tapered fingers. "I confess I have
not had new garments for some years."

Smiling to herself, Emily thought this was one hunk
who would be at his best buck naked. Now, that was
not an idea she should be entertaining at all.

Calvert missed a nail and hit his thumb for about the
tenth time since Emily had joined him on the roof. Not
that it hurt, but her presence was certainly distracting.
Maddening, he decided, was a better description.

She was wearing some sort of a knitted shirt that fit
her breasts like kid gloves and tucked into the narrow
waistband of her blue denim trousers. Whenever had
they started letting women display their virtues quite so
obviously? he wondered. Though he fully approved of
the change in costumes, these modern blokes must have
a wealth of self-restraint their ancestors had lacked.

At this very moment, he was tempted to slip up behind her and pull those lovely, full hips hard against
him. He knew just how she'd feel—firm, round and
deliciously pliable. He stifled a groan and hit his thumb
again.

"Is there a problem?" she asked.

The only difficulty was that he could not act on impulses that were as natural to Calvert as breathing.
"No. Just whacked my thumb a bit."

"Well, be careful. I'd never be able to get this job
done alone." She sat back on her haunches, balancing
herself with one hand.

"It seems to me, dear lady, that this is a task no
woman should have to endure. Instead, you should be

surrounded by silks and laces, closeted against any
hardship that would roughen your lovely hands." Soft,
warm hands he longed to hold again.

Emily laughed. "You're really going to have to join
the twentieth century, Cal. No woman likes to be closeted away or treated like a porcelain figurine that's no
good for anything except to look at."

"Of course they do." He placed another shingle in
position, considering a number of other activities he'd
like to engage in with Emily that would certainly in-
volve far more than looking. Although looking was a
pleasant experience in itself. "Women enjoy being
pampered. And it was always my pleasure, when my
allowance permitted, to give the ladies just what they
wanted. Fancy perfumes. Diamond brooches. Ball
gowns made of yards and yards of silk. Were it possible, dear lady, I would give you—"

"That's a sweet thought, Cal, but what good would
a fancy ball gown do me if the roof leaked?"

She smiled at him over her shoulder, and Calvert felt
a new tightness in his groin. *Beggar this ghost business!* He wanted her. The hunger rose up in him like a
tidal wave, sweeping past all that he knew to be true.
He wanted to feel her silky flesh pressing against him;
he wanted to taste her lovely lips and feel their soft-
ness.

And he could not *do* that.

The next nail went into the roof in a single, frustrated stroke.

THE TOWN WASN'T AS QUAINT as others in New England, nor was it as well developed with antique and

craft stores filling every nook and cranny, but Honor-ville did have its own special charm. Many of the storefronts dated back a hundred or more years and occasional sections of the main street boasted original cobbles.

Emily considered herself lucky, given the press of fall foliage tourists, to find a parking spot on the street.

Holding Becky's hand, she entered the one depart-ment store in town and headed toward the men's sec-tion. She felt a warm sense of anticipation.

She'd always enjoyed shopping for Ted's clothes, almost more than buying new things for herself. There was something very gratifying about picking out a shirt you liked and then seeing it worn by the man you loved. Not that she felt that way about Cal, she re-minded herself as she fingered a knitted, blue-and-white-striped shirt, colors that would match his eyes.

What Cal needed, she realized, was practical clothes to wear when he worked, not a signature sport shirt that would show off his eyes and emphasize the breadth of his chest. He'd done one heck of a good job that morning on the roof. Without a break, he'd laid row after row of shingles. In spite of his eccentricities, he was one hell of a good handyman.

She wondered if he had other, more intimate tal-ents, then halted the thought abruptly, almost before it was born.

Becky tugged at her jeans. "Cal says he wants this one." The child held up a red flannel shirt. "'Cause it matches his uniform."

Frowning, Emily looked down at her daughter. "He told you that's what he wanted before we left home?"

"Nuh-uh. That's what he said now."

Emily glanced around the men's department. Except for the plump saleslady, no one was around. "He's here?" she asked in a whisper. So far as Emily knew, Calvert was still working on the roof.

The child pressed the shirt into her mother's hands. "He's behind the curtain," she announced, more loudly than Emily would have liked.

The man must have hitchhiked into town, she decided, and was now hiding in the dressing room. That was the only possible way he could have arrived in the store before she had, and she certainly hadn't seen him come in the door. Yet she couldn't for the life of her remember being passed by a car on the road.

Once again she felt that now familiar disorienting sensation that made her a bit sick to her stomach—like the time she went on the Viper ride at Magic Mountain with Pete. She didn't like the feeling at all. Having two feet planted solidly on the ground was far more her style.

She hastily selected another couple of shirts and some jeans she thought would fit.

"Honey, ask Cal to try these on," she said to her daughter.

Becky did as instructed, and a few minutes later Calvert appeared.

Emily drew a quick breath. Lord, he looked good. All male and devastatingly attractive. Lean of hip, his jean-clad legs seemed to go on forever. He'd rolled the red-flannel shirtsleeves up to reveal his muscular forearms. He was smiling at her, little lines crinkling the corners of his compellingly blue eyes, and her heart did a flip-flop.

"Will this do, do you think?" he asked.

"Oh, yes." Her voice was little more than a sigh. She licked lips gone suddenly dry, and struggled against the desire to wrap her arms around his waist and rest her head on his broad chest.

Dragging her gaze away, she said, "You should have a jacket, too. The evenings are cool...."

Her hands shook as she lifted a jacket from the rack, any jacket at all. This shopping excursion had become far more intimate than she had ever expected. The visceral attraction she felt for Cal was like a living thing, sliding under her skin and boring into the pit of her stomach at the mere sight of him. She *had* to stop reacting like that.

He slipped on the coat and turned for her inspection. The back of the maroon Windbreaker was emblazoned with the words *Honorville High* in bright gold letters. Not exactly what she might have selected under other circumstances, but it would simply have to do.

"Fits well enough to have been hand-tailored," Cal conceded, studying his reflection in the mirror. "And to think you can buy such items right off the shelf. Quite amazing. You colonials have made a bit of progress, after all."

"I'm glad you approve." She approved of everything about the way Cal looked. He could easily model for *Lumberjacks Monthly*.

Straightening the lapels on the jacket, he said, "Think I will have a bit of a browse around, if you don't mind."

"Help yourself. I'll just pay for these things, and then we can be on our way."

Emily collected the tags from the clothes Cal wore and took them, along with the other merchandise she'd selected, to the salesclerk. As the woman rang up the sale, Emily noted Cal wandering up and down each aisle, looking at the displays with considerable interest. It was truly as though he'd never been in a department store before. But, of course, that wasn't possible. Perhaps it was just that he'd been broke for so long, he hadn't had a chance to go shopping.

When he joined her on the sidewalk, Emily asked, "How did you get into town so fast?"

"In your carriage." He tossed a small bundle into the back seat of the car. His uniform, she supposed. "The speed was quite frightening, I admit, but I am sure I will adjust—"

"Cal, you were *not* in my car. Becky and I would have noticed." Unless he was hiding in the trunk. Which was an absurd idea.

"As you wish, dear lady." He gave her one of those smug little grins that had her stomach and heart switching places.

"I DON'T BELIEVE in violence."

"No one will be hurt."

"We have to find some way to discourage her."

"That man she was with looked dangerous."

"He's just some bum she found to help her. He won't get in the way."

"When will you do it?"

"Tonight."

"IT'S BEDTIME, KIDS." Emily found Pete, Becky and Cal all sitting cross-legged in front of the television in the living room.

"Aw, Mom..." Peter complained.

"It's a school night for you, dear."

"But it's a good show, Mom."

"Amazing how that's always true at bedtime." Smiling, she ruffled the top of her son's blond head, his hair still damp from his bath. "Off you go—"

"It's about England. Cal's tellin' us all about where he used to live 'n' all the places he visited 'n' stuff."

Emily glanced at the screen. To her surprise, the children were actually watching a PBS program—voluntarily. She squatted down beside Becky, tugged the child into her lap and watched as the camera panned church steeples and castle keeps.

"Did you live in a castle like that, Cal?" Peter asked, pointing at the screen.

"Not so fine, I'm afraid."

"Did you know the queen?" Becky asked.

"It was King George then, lass. And aye, I met him at St. James Court."

"Did you have tea?"

Cal chuckled. "I suppose we did, though I was just a young lad at the time."

"What do you remember best?" Peter wanted to know.

"Well, now, my home and the sheep grazing across the land as far as you can see, comes to mind." He caught Emily's eye and gave her a slow, wicked wink. "And the ladies all dressed in their finery with their skirts billowing about in a breeze. Was a fine thing to catch sight of shapely ankles—"

Giving Cal a stern look, Emily pointedly switched off the TV. "The program's over, children. It's off to bed with you both."

With a minimum of fuss, she got the children tucked into bed, then returned to the living room. Cal was standing by the fireplace, his expression somber as he stared at the flames.

"Is there something wrong?" she asked.

He glanced up at the sound of her voice. The weight of a deep sadness seemed to be pressing down on him. "It is hard seeing all of the changes. I have been gone a very long time."

In spite of the improbable stories he'd told the children of meeting King George and living in a castle, Emily for some inexplicable reason didn't doubt his sincerity. "Perhaps you'll be able to go home someday."

"There is naught much to return to. They have managed to turn Witherspoon castle into a bloody museum." His mouth shaped itself into a grim line. "No doubt they taxed it into oblivion, and without a true Witherspoon heir to protect the estate..." He sighed a deep, lingering sound.

"You had no brothers?"

"Aye, Robert was the eldest."

He leaned his elbow on the oak mantel and stared unseeing into the distance. Even in jeans and a flannel shirt, he looked very much the lord of the manor. Emily knew his thoughts were a long way from New Hampshire.

Allowing him the necessary quiet for his mental journey, she eased her tired body onto a footstool. Roofing was a very physical endeavor, she decided.

The fire crackled softly.

"My brother was the ideal first son," Cal said, blinking and turning toward her once again. "Robert took his responsibilities quite seriously, to my father's delight. From the day he was born, he knew he would someday be the lord. He studied diligently. Worked with the overseer. The perfect heir. I, on the other hand..."

"Were not in the least interested."

"It was not so much that I lacked interest, there simply seemed no point. I knew the land would never be mine. As second son, I would eventually have to set out on my own. At the time, there seemed no rush."

"And you enjoyed the ladies," she ventured as a guess.

"'Tis true I have a weakness where lovely ladies are concerned." His eyes twinkled with mischief for a moment and then the sparkle faded. "After years of acting the role of wastrel younger sibling, I was indeed ill-suited to fill Robert's shoes when an unfortunate accident took his life."

"Oh, Cal. I'm sorry."

He shrugged off her sympathy. "Pity was, for once in his life Robert was having a little fun. He'd found a mistress, you see—"

"The trait must run in the family."

"—his carriage overturned, dumping them both in a heap. He never recovered from his injuries."

Emily rubbed at her aching right shoulder. "What happened to the woman?"

"She fared a bit better, but not much. My father..." Cal moved to stand behind Emily. He could see she was bone weary. Fatigue etched her beautiful face. Perhaps there was a way even a ghost could assist a lovely lady in a moment of stress. Tentatively, he placed his hands on her shoulders. Through the soft fabric, he felt the smoothness of her flesh, her soft curves and her delicacy. As his fingers massaged gently at her tired muscles, a need he could not acknowledge, much less act upon, escalated into unbearable tension.

"I am afraid my father grew quite upset when he learned I had engaged a doctor to see to the woman's injuries," he continued, girding himself against the delicious agony of denial. "Apparently, he blamed her for the accident and felt she had gotten just what she deserved."

"That's not fair." Shifting slightly, Emily decided it also wasn't fair just how wonderful Cal's hands felt kneading her flesh. Every movement of his fingers was warm and talented, as though he'd had years of experience easing a woman's aches and pains. Which, to hear his story, was probably true.

"I quite agree that she wasn't to blame, but it certainly caused a row between me and my father." He worked his thumbs in toward her spine. "After that, it seemed I never could quite please him."

"But you did try?"

"Oh, yes. It was not a situation I had expected, but the responsibility for the Witherspoon name was now mine, in succession from my father, of course."

"But if you were doing the best you could."

"'Twas never enough. Though I did have a few substantial slips, I admit."

With women, no doubt.

"Then along came the troublesome rebellion in the colonies. A rather disruptive activity. Quite a bother to His Majesty, I am sure."

His fingers worked their way up her neck. Loving his touch, Emily rotated her head.

"My father, in his wisdom, purchased a commission for me in the army. He hoped I would be able to show my mettle and redeem myself in his eyes."

"Did you?"

"Alas, no. It seems my reputation had preceded me. I was assigned only as an aide to assorted officers, none of whom were too keen on the idea. After all, I'd had no military training and was, I confess, a devout coward." He laughed dryly. "Then came the chance to prove myself here at Honorville."

"From what you've said, I gather that didn't go well."

"Being hung is not the most pleasant of experiences, I assure you. And as a traitor? No, things did not go well. And the Witherspoon name shall always carry a black mark until I can prove my innocence.''

''I'm sure you will. Someday.'' Cal's story, the flickering firelight, and the movement of his hands, lulled Emily into a warm, trancelike state. She felt deliciously at peace. And sensual. As though her body were melting at his touch. She hadn't felt that way in a very long time.

''Are you aware you're pampering me?'' she asked, allowing herself the luxury of drifting as easily as the smoke from the fireplace.

''Naturally. A woman should not work as hard as you did today.''

''Someone has to do it.''

''I regret now, dear lady, that I frightened your workmen away. Had I known you would be the one to replace them—''

''And you. I'm very grateful, Cal.''

''A trifling, my dear.''

He rotated her shoulders, easing her muscles, and for a moment she thought she felt the brush of his cheek against the top of her head. A shiver skittered down her spine.

''I had thought perhaps roses,'' he whispered, his voice a bit gravelly, ''but 'tis citrus I smell.''

''Hmm?''

''Your hair carries the fresh scent of lemon. Did you not know?''

''My shampoo...'' Lord, what was happening to her? She could feel his breath fanning across her cheek and his hands working their magic on her shoulders and back. She had the most determined urge to turn, reach up her arms and capture his mouth with hers in a hungry kiss.

It was only because she'd been alone too long, she told herself resolutely. A logical woman would not allow herself to be seduced by a near stranger, certainly not one who thought he'd grown up during the reign of King George.

The temptation to remain just where she was, and let things happen as they would, was a drugging sensation. One she forced herself to resist.

With an effort, she eased away from Cal and stood. "It's getting late."

"Aye. I suppose that is true."

His gaze was hot, burning through the fabric of her T-shirt and raising her nipples to attention, as though they were ready to salute. Her knees felt weak. Breathing was somehow a forgotten art.

Her basic sense of logic warred with a much stronger emotion. She didn't want this. Or did she? a persistent little voice inquired.

On legs that had never before failed her, though they felt strangely rubbery at the moment, she edged past Cal. "I have to get up early for Pete."

"And to continue our work on the roof."

"Yes." She choked out the sound. The feeling she was slipping out of control frightened her. Definitely an out-of-character experience. "Would you please lock up the house?" One ghost was all any woman could possibly deal with at a time.

Then she fled with as much dignity as she could muster. Her pride wouldn't allow her to let Cal know just how much his attentions affected her. Up the stairs she hurried, amazed that her legs still had the strength to carry her.

Closing the door, she leaned back against it and tried to steady her heart. Her whole world seemed to be spinning. Never in her life had any man affected her quite so strongly. And Cal, bless his heart, was decidedly the *wrong* man. Not that her body seemed aware of such subtle distinctions.

Eventually, she made her way across the room. On the bed she discovered a bag from the department store they'd visited that afternoon, the bundle she'd seen Cal carrying.

Curious, she opened the sack.

A nightie. A lacy pink number that was so skimpy it would reveal more than it hid. The kind of thing that was supposed to be worn *to* bed, and then slowly removed by a lover's hands.

"Oh, Cal..." She brought the silk to her face and rubbed the smooth fabric against her cheek. "You're not supposed to pamper me."

At that very moment, she heard a distant pop, and the lights went out.

Chapter Five

Calvert heard Emily's soft cry and bounded up the stairs three at a time. He burst into her room.

"What is it, lass?"

"Cal!" In a sudden movement, she threw herself at him. Instinctively, he wrapped his arms tightly around her delicate body. Her breasts pressed against his chest, and Cal's throat locked at the sensation. Heat exploded through his body. *God's teeth!* Had the woman no idea what she did to him?

"I'm sorry. Really." She pulled back a bit, resting her hands on his arms. He felt her fingers tremble. "It's just when the lights went out...it startled me. Then you came barging in here. I thought—" She forced an uneasy laugh. "I'm just being silly. This far from town we're bound to lose the electricity once in a while."

But that did not explain why he had heard a sound much like a musket shot just as the lights went off, he thought, or why he had heard a motorized carriage departing as he raced up the stairs. "Are you afraid of the dark, then?"

"No. Of course not."

"You have candles?"

"In the kitchen."

"I'll fetch them for you." It would give him a moment to escape her intoxicating lemon scent and put his head to rights again.

"You don't have to do that. I have a flashlight by the bed."

His gaze slid to the four-poster. In another lifetime, he would have insisted on staying. To calm her nerves, of course...and to seduce her quite thoroughly on top of that soft, elegant quilt. Just once, and very briefly, he would like to see her in that silk sleeping gown he had selected for her. Would he be able to tell, he wondered, the difference between the fabric and her equally smooth flesh? Ah, yes, most assuredly, for she would be warm and passionate. Of that he was quite confident.

If she would just give the word for him to remain.... But, alas, she wouldn't do that. Nor, should she lack such wisdom, could he accept.

Emily looked up at Cal, for the first time acutely aware they were standing in her bedroom, she in his arms, or very nearly so. The scent of wood smoke still lingered on his shirt, and she inhaled deeply, savoring the moment.

Even in the darkness she could feel the way he was looking at her. And considering her bed. Just as she was. The bunched muscles of his arms flexed, steely strong beneath her fingers, and she felt her sexual tension collide with her good sense.

Lust. Plain and simple. The sensation sizzled between them like sparklers on the Fourth of July.

"I'll be fine now," she said, her voice lacking conviction. "Thank you for coming to my rescue."

His hands slowly slipped down her arms to her fingertips. She was conscious of the strength of his hands, the rough texture, his gentleness. In a heated leap of imagination, she felt those same hands tenderly exploring her body, cupping her breasts, smoothing her flesh, which was growing warm at the mere thought.

He held her for a heart-stopping moment while her mind provided a hundred erotic images, then he released his grip on her fingers. "A gentleman's duty, my dear. Rescuing fair damsels in distress."

He stepped out the door, his dark shadow—broad-shouldered and lean of hip—vanishing silently into the night.

Emily sagged onto the edge of the bed.

Oh, my. What in heaven's name was happening to her?

Her heart fluttered as wildly as a hummingbird's, but with many more times the volume of blood pumping through her veins. She should be glad she'd had enough sense to back off, even when she'd made the foolhardy, illogical mistake of flying into Cal's arms when he'd appeared at her door.

But dammit all, *glad* wasn't what she was feeling. Frustration was much closer to the truth. Needy. Vulnerable. And oh so feminine.

Cal wasn't the kind of man she'd dreamed about finding. In fact, he was about as far from Ted and his conservative engineer's approach to life as she could imagine. Most of the men she'd dated before marriage had been much the same.

If the truth were known, she never would have *dared* to fantasize about a man like Cal—a bearded, mysterious man who could tap into her sexuality just by being in the same room. A man who would actually want to *pamper* her. *Protect* her. What utter nonsense. In this century, such a man didn't exist.

She fingered the lacy nightie on the bed next to her. It would feel so wonderful to...

Absolute madness! She, the most logical person she knew, wanted to be with Calvert T. Witherspoon, the most red-blooded *ghost* she'd ever met. She would have laughed aloud except for the startling intensity of her feelings.

Trying not to think, she slowly undressed and slipped the gown over her head. She felt alternately hot and cold as the fabric settled around her.

She really should have thanked him for his gift, she rationalized. The small courtesy would only take a moment.

Using her flashlight, she walked down the hallway and quietly mounted the stairs. The carpet was rough on her bare feet, her breathing irregular. A shockingly wanton urge, totally unfamiliar, drove her upward.

At his closed door, she knocked softly. When there was no response, she opened it a few inches.

He was there. She could feel him across the distance. Watching her. Wanting her. The feeling was palpable, it had weight and color, a shimmering path of thought and need that flowed between them.

"I wanted to thank you for the nightgown." She trembled with the tight thrill of anticipation. His bed was narrow. She knew that. But it didn't matter. She simply wanted to be there with him. If he would only say the word.

A pause. Longer than she would have liked.

"It was but a small token of my esteem, my dear. Regretfully, I was forced by the lack of funds to add the cost to your tab, but the woman was amenable. I trust you do not—"

"It was the thought. Thank you." He was so still, lying there on the bed. No more than a shadowed silhouette in the silver moonlight. If only he would...

She swallowed against the dryness in her mouth. "Well, goodnight."

The pause was longer, wavering in the air like heat waves on a summer day. Wasn't he going to invite her in? Dear God, had she misjudged his actions, given Cal thoughts that were hers alone? That possibility sliced into her like a carving knife slipping from her grasp to cut through her flesh.

"Good night, Emily."

As the door closed, Cal strangled the blanket with his fist. By all that was holy, she wanted him. Emily Morrell *wanted* him as much as he desired her. And there was not a thing this side of heaven or hell he could do about it.

The realization was as bitter as sour ale in his mouth.

"IT'S GOING TO TAKE three or four days to repair?"

Emily craned her neck at the power company repairman perched near the top of the pole.

"At least that, ma'am. We'll have to send to Concord for a new transformer." Adjusting his safety belt, he started back down the pole. His tools clanked in the cool morning air. "Somebody sure didn't want you to have no electricity."

"Somebody?" She glanced at Cal, who was standing nearby watching the repairman. With his thumbs tucked in his jean pockets, he looked for all the world like a cowboy right out of the old West. A very attractive one, at that, and sexy as hell. The denim fabric tugged snugly across his thighs. His wide-legged stance was blatantly masculine, making Emily think about things she shouldn't.

The young man dropped the last few feet to the ground and unharnessed himself. "Looks to me like somebody pried open the box, then planted a cherry bomb, or some such, inside. Made a real mess. Turned all the wiring into confetti." He held out his hand to show her a small fragment of red paper and burned pieces of wire.

"What is a cherry bomb?" Cal asked.

"It's a big firecracker," she answered. Her forehead tightened into a frown. "I thought they were outlawed."

"Sure they are," the repairman said, "but folks bring 'em back from Mexico or Vegas. Heard aboot a kid gettin' his hand blowed off last year. Nasty business."

"But who would have—"

"This transformer's fixed up just for your electrical service, ma'am. Nobody else is on the line. I reckon whoever did this doesn't like you much." A blush colored his cheeks as he gave her a patently approving look. "Darn shame, I'd say."

She didn't react to the young man's appreciative expression, but it did help rebuild her ego after the prior evening's fiasco. "Surely it was just some sort of juvenile prank."

"Looks more like vandalism to me, ma'am. Not somethin' kids would do on a lark."

Emily felt prickles of anxiety along the back of her neck. "Guess I'll have to report it to the sheriff." Though she didn't have a high degree of confidence in the local police establishment.

"If you would be willing, lad," Cal said, "you could save Mrs. Morrell the bother."

"Huh?" The young man's gaze darted to Cal and back to Emily again. "How's that?"

"If you would contact the necessary officials for her, it would save her the burden. She has, of course, found this situation quite discomforting."

"Oh, yeah, sure. I'll do that for you, ma'am," the young man agreed. "The power company don't exactly like folks blowing up their equipment."

Emily smiled. Cal was certainly a persuasive man, without even trying to be. She doubted anyone could resist his silver tongue.

"Thank you," she said. "That would save me the trouble."

With a shrug, the repairman packed up his tools, then drove off in his van.

Cal leaned back against the rock fence and folded his arms across his chest. "I don't like the sound of this, Emily."

"Neither do I," she conceded. She also didn't like the fact that he had rejected her overtures last night. She couldn't have been more blatant about her interest. But then, perhaps he was wiser than she. Whatever the case, it had hurt. More deeply than she cared to admit.

"Have you . . . that is, do you have any enemies?"

"I haven't been here long enough to—" She shrugged. "Sometimes in town I get the feeling no one wants me around. I really haven't the vaguest idea why not."

"Maybe you ought to try to find out."

"I suppose." She tucked her fingertips into the hip pockets of her jeans. Cal was wearing his flannel shirt again this morning. Red was definitely his color. It made his eyes appear intensely blue. "I've got Becky enrolled in a preschool art class that starts tomorrow. She's so bored alone around the house with no children to play with, I thought it would give her something to do. Maybe while she's in class I could do some checking."

"That sounds like a good strategy."

"But there's the roof. I don't want to leave you with the whole job."

"I'll manage." He gave her another one of those confident grins that made Emily regret he hadn't taken her up on her offer. She barely stifled her sigh of frustration. No good would come of letting him know just how anxious she'd been.

It wasn't that sex had ever been all that important to her. The opposite, in fact. But with Cal she sensed it would be different. More erotic. More sensitive. More thoroughly involving.

Darn it all. It didn't look like she'd ever find out.

As they walked up the drive to the house, she forced her thoughts back to the vandalism. The general current of animosity she'd felt from the townspeople had evidently turned mean. But why? She and her B and B were no possible threat to anyone in Honorville. From what she'd learned in her research, there was plenty of need for more tourist accommodations in the area. At least, at peak season that was true. So fear of competition couldn't be the reason someone would want her business to fail.

She shook her head and expelled a long sigh. Answers would have to wait until she could get into town the next day. In her experience, libraries and librarians contained a wealth of information. She'd start there. Meanwhile she'd ignore the nervous knot in her stomach. The vandalism was, after all, only one step above a harmless prank. She had nothing to fear.

"Come on, lass. It's not like you to be discouraged." Cal walked up the porch steps beside her.

"I'm more puzzled than discouraged." Both about the vandalism and why Cal hadn't taken advantage of the opportunity she'd offered last night.

"What you need is a good cuppa to soothe you, lass. That's what my mum always used to do when she had a vexing problem to solve."

"Your mum?" Whatever else Cal might be, he was one hundred percent British.

"Aye, she was a lovely lady. Full of spice and vinegar, with a good deal of sweetness thrown in. Much like you."

Emily registered the compliment but didn't know quite how to react. He was definitely the hardest man to read she'd ever met. "Perhaps you're right about the tea," she said. "Care to join me?"

"It would be my pleasure." He held open the screen door for Emily and, with a sweep of his arm, ushered her inside. The perfect gentleman. *Damn!* Just her luck.

When they reached the kitchen, they found what closely resembled chaos.

Chapter Six

"Becky! What on earth are you doing?"

Every can and jar had been hauled out of the cupboards and stacked on top of the maple breakfast table. The contents of Emily's purse were strewn around the room. In the middle of the mess, Becky stood smiling up at Emily. The child was wearing a pair of her mother's high-heel sandals, garishly applied lipstick and, of all things, the skimpy pink nightgown pulled on over her play clothes. Emily nearly choked from embarrassment.

"I been playing I went to the grocery store," Becky announced. "I bought all this stuff."

"Did you have to buy quite so much?" Emily groaned. And choose Cal's gift as a costume?

Cal scooped Becky into his arms. His eyes twinkled with mischief. "Well now, lass, is that not a lovely gown you are wearing."

"It's my mommy's."

"I imagine it would fit a bit different on her." He lifted one of the loose straps back onto Becky's shoulder.

"It's real pretty."

"It is that, lass. It is indeed."

"Do English ladies wear these?"

He caught Emily's eye, and she felt heat color her cheeks. She knew he was imagining what she would look like in the nightie. *You missed your chance, fella,* she thought grimly. She didn't think he'd gotten a good look at her in the darkness outside his door last night. The way he slowly raised a speculative eyebrow, maybe she should have opened the door wider.

"Perhaps they wear such attire now," Cal told Becky. "It's been a while since I have inquired."

"Honey, I want you to go upstairs and put my nightgown away just where you found it." Next time Emily would hide it at the bottom of the drawer. "And be careful taking it off."

"But I'm not finished shopping," the child objected.

"Yes, you are. Upstairs with you. Then you can look at your 'Sesame Street' books." She gave her daughter a stern look. "And next time you want to play dress-up with my clothes, you ask me."

Becky's lower lip puckered.

Cal eased the child to the floor. "Off you go." He turned her in the direction of the door and gave her an affectionate swat on her bottom that sent her on her way.

Picking up a couple of cans, Emily sighed. "I can hardly wait until she starts school next year."

"But you will miss her, I imagine."

"Probably. But I'm more than willing to make the sacrifice. Kindergarten is unquestionably a mother's best friend."

Cal stooped to pick up some of the debris that had escaped from Emily's oversize reticule. He fingered a card that contained a miniature portrait of Emily as well as her name. As he read the printed words, a knot formed in his gut. Memories assailed him.

Another woman came to mind. Blond. The face of an angel, with rosy lips and a nose that tipped up at the end. A soft, silken body. A woman he had loved and who had betrayed him. One who very much resembled Emily Morrell.

He rested his hand on the kitchen table to steady himself and watched as she replaced the canned goods on a shelf.

"You are Alice," he said, his voice thick.

Emily glanced over her shoulder. "That's my middle name. Rebecca's, too. How did you... Oh, my driver's license."

"A strange coincidence."

"What's that?" She stacked the last can in the cupboard, shut the door, and turned to see what had brought such a troubled tone to Cal's voice. Deep furrows grooved his forehead.

"Do you perchance recall my mentioning the wench who had been my downfall?"

"I suppose." Amazing how easily she forgot that Cal thought of himself as a ghost. So much of the time he seemed ... normal.

Confusion fuzzing the corners of her brain, she took her driver's license and slipped it back into her wallet.

"Her name was Alice. Alice Henderson."

Emily's hands went very still. "You knew Alice Henderson?" Perhaps he'd only found her name somewhere in the house, or heard the tales of Emily's ancestor in the town. "She was my great-great-great-grandmother, removed about ten times. She married a Barton, which was my maiden name. It's a family tradition that her first-born female descendants carry her name."

With one finger, Cal lifted Emily's chin. She felt the searching intensity of his gaze travel slowly across her face, touching, in a curiously caressing way, first her eyes, then her nose and cheeks. Finally his eyes settled on her mouth, lingering there for many long moments. Somewhere low in her body, she registered a throbbing sensation. Her pulse rate accelerated. Lord, he was going to kiss her. *At last*.

"Yes, I can see the resemblance."

See? All Emily could do was feel—his warm breath on her face and the riotous, illogical desire that sapped the strength from her legs. "Resemblance?" she echoed, her voice cracking.

"You are different, yet the same. In the eyes, the nose and most especially…your mouth. Strange I had not seen it before."

Her tongue swept her lips to moisten them. "Cal, what are you talking about?" Why was he talking at all? At this particular moment, she'd have preferred a little action.

He touched her hair, playing his fingers through the short, curly strands. "Hers was longer, a blond that was a shade or two darker, and not so fine."

Trying to fight the tremble that shook her, Emily placed her hand on Cal's chest. His heart beat hard against her palm. Hers was thrumming equally hard in her throat. "You're talking crazy, Cal. There's no possible way you can know what Alice Henderson looked like. There were no pictures, no paintings—"

"I was here, Emily. When she lived, we were lovers. Then she betrayed me."

Emily's hand dropped to her side. She took a step back. What insanity within her caused such an incredible attraction to this strange man? she wondered.

"You still do not believe who and what I am," he said.

She shook her head. "We need to get back to the roof—"

"No!" He took her by the shoulders, his fingers biting almost painfully into her flesh. His body radiated tension and self-restraint barely held in check, yet she didn't feel any fear for her safety. Only a deep sympathy that seemed to reach past the boundaries of time, as though she was connected in some unfathomable way to the Alice Henderson who had once lived here. And loved.

"You must listen, Emily. After all these years, I have to make one person understand. You, the one person who carries some piece of Alice Henderson within you, must believe me."

Good sense and logic warred with another feeling Emily couldn't define. She ought to send him out of the house, hire roofers from Concord and be done with him. Calvert T. Witherspoon—and his mental health— weren't her responsibility. Yet at some basic level she already believed him. And that fact was totally beyond her understanding.

"I'll make us some tea," she said. "Why don't you start from the beginning?"

He visibly relaxed, his forehead smoothing as he released his firm grip on her shoulders. He pulled out a chair at the kitchen table.

"You have heard the first of the story—my commissioning at my father's behest and then my assignment here at Honorville. There was a great deal of support for the Crown in the New Hampshire colony."

She raised a questioning eyebrow. "Tories?"

"Aye. That's what they were called by the rebels." Sitting down, he thoughtfully adjusted the spoon in the sugar bowl on the table. "I was sent here to organize the locals into a spy ring that would track our opponents. I was to report back to my superiors about troop movements, enlistments and morale. That sort of thing."

Putting a pot of water on the stove, Emily asked, "Was Alice Henderson a British sympathizer?" She'd never considered her family's role in the Revolutionary War, always assuming they must have been loyal Americans. It was like discovering a colorful horse thief among her ancestors.

"I believed she was loyal to the Crown. She had four brothers, and all of them, save the youngest who was but twelve at the time, enlisted in my enterprise. Obviously, I was deceived, and my honor betrayed."

Honor. That seemed to be Cal's touchstone. Had he also treated Alice Henderson honorably? she wondered. Strange she didn't feel a jealous twinge toward her ancestor. It hardly seemed appropriate when the woman had been dead for two centuries. Not that she could possibly believe his story.

"How were you betrayed?" she asked.

"I honestly do not know. I had knowledge of our own troop movements, though I swear by all that is holy, I did not reveal a single fact to any other human—not even to Alice. Yet somehow..." He raked his fingers through his hair, dislodging the dark, wavy strands in a way that made him look as though he'd just awakened from a long, restless sleep. Or had thoroughly enjoyed a night of making love.

Emily forced the thought aside.

"One of our patrols was ambushed not far from here. There was significant loss of life. The officer in charge was wounded. After a brief investigation by my superiors, I was blamed. By then, you see, the Hendersons were known as rebels and I had consorted with the enemy."

Emily's heart went out to Cal. He looked so troubled, it was impossible not to believe *he* was convinced of his story. "But if you had told no one—"

"Alice confessed to my superior, or so he said. The major had never liked me and was an arrogant son-of-a—" He clenched his fists on the tabletop. "The man absolutely delighted in telling the court-martial tribunal how Alice had told him everything. How she had seduced me. How she had used my weakness for her and turned it to the rebel cause, learning details that I had never shared with anyone. It was all a lie. Everything! Yet without even adjourning, the court convicted me. Then ordered me hung."

Placing a cup of tea in front of Cal, Emily covered his fisted hand with hers. He was warm and sturdy and very much alive. Not a ghost, she told herself, fighting the way her heart and mind kept vacillating back and forth to control her thoughts. "And you're still trying to prove your innocence."

"Aye. There's a diary, you see. Alice told me she wrote in it every night, though I never saw the book myself. It is still here somewhere. If I could but find—"

"Cal, after so many years . . . it could be anywhere. Or nowhere at all. She could have taken it with her when she moved. It could have been lost. Someone else could have—"

"No, it is still here. Somewhere. I know it is. She told me once it was well hidden. She and her family left in haste, and I doubt she had time to retrieve the book. I believed her then that no one else would ever find it, and I still do."

"But you've looked—"

"For two hundred years." His fingers curled over hers and the corners of his mouth lifted into a sexy grin. "I do not give up any more easily than you do, lass."

She laughed a throaty sound. "Then I guess I'd better help you find the diary if I ever want Henderson House to be free of its resident ghost."

"You would help me, then?"

Agreeing to a bargain with a ghost, Emily squeezed his hand. "If that's what you'd like." What would she do if they actually found the diary? Would that prove he was a ghost? And what if he left her? That impossible thought brought a strange, hollow feeling to her chest.

Later that afternoon, as she prepared dinner, Emily noticed the absence of Cal's steady hammering on the roof. She glanced out the window to find her handyman and Peter practicing the fine art of self-defense on the front lawn.

Moving agilely, Cal dodged Peter's roundhouse swing. "Easy, lad. Wait for the right chance."

The boy advanced again.

"That's right," Cal encouraged. "Keep your right hand up to ward off their blows." With an open hand, he demonstrated how weak Peter's defenses were.

"Don't let him hit you," Becky encouraged from the sidelines.

Giving his sister a sidelong glance, Pete renewed his efforts. This time he managed to deflect Cal's attack and landed a slanting uppercut himself.

Cal staggered back in mock surprise. "Now you are catching on. 'Tis a good student you are." He tousled the boy's hair and they went at it again.

Fascinated, Emily watched for a moment more, aware of both Cal's patience with her son and his athletic grace, as well. He was a man who would provide a perfect counterpoint to any woman. *For her,* she mentally corrected, in spite of knowing she shouldn't feel that way.

She smiled. Pete needed a man to look up to. How strange that both she and her children were drawn to the company of a man who thought of himself as a two-hundred-year-old ghost. What a totally implausible situation.

The sheriff's car wheeled onto the driveway and interrupted Emily's thoughts.

She dried her hands on a tea towel and went out to meet him. The man had certainly taken his own sweet time about investigating the vandalism report. Hard to believe the police were all that busy in Honorville.

"Afternoon, ma'am." Sheriff Belinger lifted his hat. "Heard tell you've had more problems."

"We're going to be without electricity for several days," she said.

"Sorry to hear that. Sounds like kids—"

"The repairman thought it was more than just a childish prank."

"Well, ya know how ornery kids are these days." His gaze focused on Cal. "Then again, maybe your prowler came back. Or the Henderson ghost."

"No, sheriff. It wasn't a ghost that set off a cherry bomb in the transformer." Emily was Cal's alibi, both before and after the lights went off. The memory of her wanton behavior still had the power to bring a tightness to her stomach.

"I believe," Cal said, "that the perpetrator of the crime departed rather hurriedly in a motorized carriage."

The sheriff cocked his head. "Motorized—"

"He means a car."

"That so?" Frowning, the sheriff took a notebook from his shirt pocket and asked, "Did you get a license number or model?"

"Alas, I only heard the vehicle, as I was...otherwise occupied."

The notebook went back into the sheriff's pocket. "Not much to go on, I'm afraid."

"I suppose not," Emily agreed, disgusted. Heaven forbid the sheriff might check for fingerprints or find out who in town had access to cherry bombs. He was definitely not treating this case as a big-time investigation. For a moment she considered asking Cal to do one of his vanishing tricks, and then thought better of the idea. But it would certainly have gotten the policeman's attention.

"Maybe you should think aboot moving oot till all this can be sorted through," the officer suggested.

"My ancestors managed just fine without electricity. We'll get along." Everyone in town was certainly anxious to get her out of the house.

After the sheriff left, Emily turned to Cal. "I didn't know you heard a car last night."

"I didn't want to worry you, my dear."

"Do you think I should be afraid?"

A breeze rustled the tops of the trees and a blizzard of colorful leaves rained down on the driveway. "I intend to keep my sabre at the ready, dear lady. Just to be on the safe side."

Cal looped his arm around Emily's delicate shoulders. He silently vowed he would let no harm come to her or her children. Though he could not give her more than that, he would stake all that was his to protect her.

"THERE ARE SOME advantages to no electricity."

After a candlelit dinner, Emily sat with her legs curled under her on the couch. Cal sat opposite her in his favorite wing chair. He'd found a pipe, and the fragrant tobacco smoke drifted up through the light cast by an old lantern. In a casual, thoroughly masculine gesture, he shifted the pipe stem so it teased at his lips, drawing her gaze. He drew a breath and exhaled a slow stream of smoke that formed itself into a circle. Though the whole process had taken only a moment, Emily felt quite mesmerized.

His lips. So mobile and expressive. How would they feel kissing her? she wondered. And his beard? Rough? Or soft against her cheek? She'd never kissed a bearded man. No doubt her curiosity was simply working overtime.

"But electricity does seem a wondrous invention," he said. "A work-saver, I should imagine."

"True. But this is the first night I can remember in years when the kids didn't battle about what to watch on television."

A low chuckle rumbled up from his chest and teased across Emily's flesh. She rubbed at her arms.

"Cold, are you?"

"No, not really." The fire was doing a perfectly adequate job of keeping the room warm. The problem had more to do with her persistent fantasies about Cal. Just now she'd been considering how pleasant it would be to have these cozy evenings together go on for a long, long time. He was a good companion—even-tempered and considerate. She valued that in a man. The thought of him pampering her for the next fifty years or so had considerable appeal. As did far more intimate activities they could enjoy together. Those images kept popping into her mind at the least little thing—an accidental brush of their bodies, a certain look in his eye. The whole situation had her constantly on the brink of arousal. A smoldering heat low in her body. Persistent breathlessness. Breasts that were hypersensitive to the least little pressure.

"Shall we get on with it?"

Her muscles went taut. "Now?"

"It seems as good a time as any to renew my search for the diary."

"Oh, that." Emily did a rather poor job of covering her disappointment. Where had her reason fled?

"Unless you would rather not."

"Now is fine." She uncurled herself and placed her feet on the floor. "Let's start by trying to think our way through this logically." She used to be very good at step-by-step deduction, a skill she'd apparently misplaced somewhere between California and New Hampshire. "Where have you looked so far?"

He pulled on the pipe, his sensuous lips fitting around the stem, and exhaled a puff of smoke. "Everywhere I could think of."

"How old was Alice?"

"Seventeen, as I recall."

"Young."

His lips quirked up and little lines formed at the corners of his eyes. "Aye, but a woman for all of that."

This time jealousy did tweak Emily. The woman had been half her age. The thought made her feel ancient at thirty-five. "We needn't go into any details. It seems to me such a *young* girl would most likely keep her di-

ary right in her room, where she could write in it every
night.''

''That is indeed where I started my search. I found
nothing.''

''Perhaps a hidey-hole in the wall, a loose floor-
board?''

''I have walked through every wall in the house. So
far, all I have found are rusty nails.''

''But surely in a place as old as this there must be
dozens of unexpected nooks and crannies, secret passageways, peepholes.'' If she could get him to admit
that, she'd be a long way toward proving Cal wasn't
even close to being a ghost.

Good grief! Even her thoughts had become incon-
gruous. One moment she believed his tale and the next
she knew it was impossible. For the time being, she'd
simply go with the flow, she thought. She rubbed her
fingertips at the niggling headache threatening her
temple.

''I suspect, my dear, you have been reading too many
romantic novels. I assure you, Henderson House con-
tains no such secret places.''

Pity. That would have made her life much easier.
''Well...those romantic books you're talking about
always have a loose brick in the fireplace. Have you
tried that?''

His pipe clattered into the ashtray and he leaped to
his feet. ''Good lord, Emily. You are brilliant! Absolutely brilliant.''

In two long strides he was at the fireplace. Picking
up the poker, he methodically tapped the bricks one at
a time, working his way across the hearth and then up

the sides. The sound never varied from an off-key twang.

When he began reaching well up into the chimney, so intent on his search he even ignored the heat of the fire, Emily stood and went to him. She placed her hand on his shoulder.

"It's no use, Cal. She never would have been able to hide the diary up so high."

He sat back on his haunches. "I had so hoped...." He looked up at her, and Emily's heart constricted at the determination she saw in his eyes and the grim set of his jaw. "I was the black sheep of the family, you see. If I could only prove to my father..."

"Hush, now," she whispered. His pain was real; whether he was a man or a ghost, it didn't matter. Willingly, she accepted some part of his burden. She cupped her hand against the back of his head, her fingers lacing through his ebony hair. He flattened his whiskered cheek against her abdomen, wrapping his arms around her waist. She cherished the feeling of closeness, the press of his body against hers. For a moment she experienced a sensation of déjà vu, as though she had held Calvert like this before, perhaps in some other life. But, of course, that wasn't possible.

"I know you'll find the diary. It was left where only you would know where to look." Even to her own ears, her voice sounded strangely distant and unfamiliar, as though shifting through a time warp she couldn't possibly understand.

A low, guttural sound vibrated through Calvert as hunger knotted fiercely in his body, making his muscles bunch. *By damn!* He wanted this woman. He wanted to taste her heat, to find her honeyed womanhood hidden in the thatch of golden curls that lay but inches from his lips. His need was a torturous thing, flaying him with each gentle stroke of her fingers. The injustice of it all tore at him as if he were a man being pulled apart on the rack. Her scent taunted him; the soft swell of her breasts teased from just beyond where he dared to explore.

He *had* to gather his wits about him or surely madness would follow.

Slowly, he let his hands settle across her hips and follow the curve to her thighs. He felt her tremble and knew he dared not venture more, for her sake as well as his. He delved deep into his store of self-restraint.

"We need a new plan, I fear," he said, standing. "Once again the diary has eluded me." He looked into her dazed, sultry eyes. She hid little from him, least of all her own need. Calvert cursed himself for failing her.

"Logically..." She visibly struggled with her own torment. "We should begin...somewhere in the house and work our way room by room. We'll just have to cover every bit of ground even if you've looked there before."

"Should we start with the attic or the basement, do you suppose?"

She hesitated, her breasts heaving as she drew shallow breaths. Her pulse fluttered at her throat. "The attic, I think."

They carried two lanterns up the stairs to the storage room. A jumble of old furniture, trunks and general debris crammed themselves under the low ceiling.

The attic had held in the heat of the day and the stale air felt heavy and musty. Emily drew a deep breath to steady herself.

"I've always been amazed that everything has been left so untouched," she said. The strength had finally returned to her legs, and with the need to actually search for the diary, she felt somewhat more in control. The intimate way Cal had held her, and then so easily let her go, had shaken her foundations. The man was sending out mixed messages she couldn't begin to translate. It left her feeling very unsure of herself.

"In California," she mused, "a house like this would have been stripped bare within days after the owners left." She ran her fingertips through the dust on top of a solid oak chest of drawers. There hadn't yet been time to investigate all the hidden treasures in the house.

"Over the years a few brave souls have trespassed. Naturally, I frightened them off."

"I hate to break the news to you, Cal, but you're not a very scary ghost."

He raised his eyebrows. "No? As I recall, you ran from me on our first meeting."

"I admit the sword trick made me a little nervous. But I think overall you qualify more as a poltergeist." Kneeling, she lifted the lid of a wooden trunk. The hinges creaked.

"And all this time I thought I had finally discovered an occupation for which I was eminently suited."

Emily thought Cal's calling was more closely related to being a ladies' man. "If you hadn't been forced to serve in the army, what would you have done with your life?'' The trunk appeared to contain women's clothing, each garment carefully wrapped in yellowed tissue paper.

''Managed my father's estates.'' He shifted a broken high chair out of the way and peered behind the chest. ''My father had rather large agricultural holdings, though I confess I had no great talent for knowing which crops would be profitable or how the price of wool might vary. His other business ventures were even more dreadfully boring. The work entailed little else than that which a clerk could do. He accused me of having no interest in any of his enterprises except the tavern, where I did tend to spend considerable time.''

''Really? Then maybe you're a natural-born innkeeper.''

He leaned his elbow on the chest. ''I had not considered that possibility. However, more than once I served as barkeep when old Amos was in his cups. I found it a pleasant way to while away a few hours.''

She supposed so. In fact, it was easy to imagine Cal serving her guests aperitifs in the living room, then charming them all during dinner. He seemed to know a good deal of the history of New England, at least from the British point of view. A resident ghost-cum-English-army-captain would certainly bring in the crowds. Perhaps she ought to give the concept some serious thought.

She shook out one of the dresses. Unlike the others she'd lifted from the trunk, which had been quite ordinary, this one was of fine powder-blue muslin, with a row of lace edging the square-cut neckline. Wondering who might have once worn the dress, she fingered the soft fabric and felt a strange shifting and settling inside her body.

"It was to have been her wedding gown," Cal said.

Emily's head came up in surprise.

"I sent a compatriot to Boston to search out the finest fabric he could find."

"For Alice?"

Lips unsmiling, he nodded.

"She never wore it?"

"Nay. She sewed it in secret, as we did not have her family's approval, or so she said." He shrugged. "Now I know they never would have agreed to her marriage to a British officer. Not when their sympathies were with the colonies."

"But if she wanted to marry you—"

"No doubt it was not the first time a man had been duped by a clever wench."

Emily didn't think that was the case. The dress was too carefully, too lovingly made with fine, tiny stitches. No woman would go to that much trouble just to carry off a charade.

"Try it on, lass. Let's see how you look in it."

"I couldn't—"

"Of course you can." Taking Emily's arm, he helped her to her feet. "I have seen you in naught but those trousers, and it would do a man good to see you dressed as of old."

"You don't like my jeans?" she laughed.

He stood back and gave her a slow, appraising look. "Even the young man this morning who clambered like a monkey up the pole knew you were worth a closer study. But it is sometimes what is hidden that drives a man wild rather than the shape that can be seen.''

Feeling heat creep up her neck, she said, "You have a silver tongue, Captain Witherspoon.'' Wicked eyes, too, that told a woman just what she wanted to hear, even when she shouldn't listen. "Little wonder you were so popular with the ladies.''

"At last you have identified the occupation that truly suits me best.'' Grinning, he glanced around the attic. "Behind that screen will provide the privacy you need.''

Her gaze followed his to a small partition tucked back in the shadows. Her first inclination was to fold the dress and put it back in the trunk. On the other hand, she rationalized, few women had a chance to wear a gown that an ancestor had once intended for her wedding. A wedding that by all rights should have taken place, and didn't.

What grief and sadness Alice Henderson must have experienced at the loss of her lover. Holding the woman's dress, Emily could feel the young woman's pain knotting her stomach and weighing down on her shoulders. And what strange circumstances had led to their separation....

An urge more compelling than Cal's request drove Emily to the far side of the screen. Her hands shook as she pulled off her shirt and jeans, then lifted the dress over her head. The sleeves were tight to the elbow and then flared; the low-cut neckline pulled tight as she laced up the front opening. Her mouth was dry and her pulse beat wildly in her throat.

When she stepped from behind the screen, she heard Cal draw a quick breath. The lantern lights cast evocative shadows across his face, darkening his beard and reflecting like spots of fire in his eyes. The way his jeans fit as snugly as breeches and the color of his flannel shirt made it seem as though he still wore his dress uniform, as he would have for his wedding day.

He held out his hands in invitation. She noticed his fingers trembled almost as badly as hers.

As she went to him, she felt the fluttering sensation of butterfly wings in her stomach, just like a bride would experience when she walked down the aisle to meet her groom.

Chapter Seven

"Lovely." The word escaped Calvert's throat in a hoarse whisper. "I dreamed of seeing Alice like this. Now I have found you."

"I'm afraid she was a size smaller."

His gaze dipped to the expanse of creamy flesh thrusting from the confines of the bodice. "Your endowments are quite satisfactory. I have admired them often."

"You have?"

"Aye. Did you not know?"

A blush rose up her neck. "I wasn't sure."

"There is much about you that is worthy of a poet's praise."

"You've never said."

"Even now, I should have kept my silence." He raised both of her hands to his lips and brushed kisses against the backs of her fingers. A warmth curled through his body, more than lust and far more dangerous and unattainable. "We should dance." The wedding dance that never happened.

"There's no music."

"I believe, with us the music is already in our hearts." A dangerous urge was on him to touch her, hold her—foolhardy, perhaps, but an irresistible urge. "Do you not hear it, as well?"

Her response was but a sweet sigh.

At his touch on her back, Emily slid her hand slowly up his arm to his shoulder. His eyes were as dark as midnight and filled with desire. She felt a heavy, thrumming response low in her belly. "The attic's so crowded. There's no room—"

"Close your eyes. We will imagine . . . and remember our first dance together."

Following his softly spoken instructions, Emily found herself in a ballroom. Mirrored sconces holding aromatic candles cast circles of light across elegantly attired guests. Long gowns of taffeta and satin whispered in rhythm to quietly playing violins. Distinguished gentlemen in dark suits and straight-backed officers in military uniforms led their partners around the highly polished floor. The scent of perfume varied with each passing couple.

She swayed, moving with Cal through the imaginary dancers, feeling the heat of his palm at the small of her back, the rippling muscles at his shoulder, and the way his tapered fingers enclosed her much smaller hand. Moisture formed between her thighs. Her breathing grew shallow and labored.

Their first dance. So formal and dignified. So unlike anything she'd ever experienced. She could go on dancing like this the rest of her life.

"All these years," Cal said in a low, intimate voice, "with nothing but loneliness and the memory of betrayal to keep me company, I continued to dream. There were times when I welcomed intruders, for it gave me someone to haunt and kept my mind occupied."

She opened her eyes. "Are you glad you didn't frighten me off?"

"Aye." The corners of his lips quirked. "But you may not always feel the same."

"I think...I think I will."

"That may not be wise, Emily." Perversely, he wanted to warn her off. They had no future together. They were caught in but a moment of time where the past and present had crossed. Yet he couldn't find the courage to release her.

"I've been wise all my life. Perhaps it's time for a change."

Her beguiling eyes, darkening to indigo in the lamplight, spoke volumes as her gaze lingered on his mouth. He ached to accept what she offered with a fury he had never before experienced. She edged closer until her pleated skirt brushed against his thighs like a hot sun burning through the fabric. Her hands were damp, or perhaps it was his own heat he felt. He longed to caress the swell of her breasts that heaved with each shallow intake of air; he agonized over the desire to bury his face between their sweet, soft pillows.

A man should not be tested this way, he thought. To be offered a feast and be unable to partake was the most cruel of punishments. Far worse than the feel of the rope tightening around his neck.

For the first time in two hundred years, Calvert T. Witherspoon wished to God he would never find the damn diary. But his family's honor would not allow him the luxury of that weakness. Not even if his failure to clear his name would mean he could spend the rest of eternity with Emily.

. He fought the constriction in his throat. "It is not always well to seek change, my dear, unless you know all of the consequences." Reluctantly, he released her.

Her chin wobbled and she abruptly turned away. "We're wasting time." She clipped her words, and Calvert cursed himself for hurting her.

"If we're going to find that diary," she said with ill-concealed confusion, "we'd better get on with it."

THE HONORVILLE LIBRARY smelled a lot like her attic.

Emily quickly shoved the thought aside. She didn't want to deal with last night. Never before had she considered herself as having a fragile ego, but Cal was certainly making her rethink that assessment.

He was only a man, she reminded herself sternly. If he didn't want her, so what? She wasn't one of those women who felt incomplete without some guy always hanging around. Even in her marriage, she'd been independent. She was perfectly content on her own, with her children to love and her business to run.

Straightening her shoulders, she marched up to the librarian's desk. At this point, she'd only concern herself with determining who was so anxious to run her out of town.

She couldn't have been more surprised to find a black woman working behind the desk. She was probably fifty, a slim, well-built woman, immaculately dressed, with just a trace of gray in her hair. The nameplate identified her as Irene Carver.

"I'm new in Honorville," Emily began, "and I thought I'd like to learn something about the community. Could you recommend some books?"

"Of course." She spoke in the soft voice typical of librarians. "Is your interest primarily in history or contemporary affairs?"

"Some of both." Like British captains left over from the Revolutionary War, and vandals who sabotage transformers.

Emily followed Ms. Carver to the history section, where the librarian selected an oversize volume from the shelf.

"A whole book on the history of Honorville?" she asked.

"Oh, yes. Most communities have an historical society. There is a publisher that specializes in producing materials that the societies sell as fund-raisers. Particularly in New England, they are quite popular."

"And wordy." Emily weighed the heavy book in her hand.

With a serene smile, Ms. Carver said, "The people of Honorville do seem inordinately proud of their history."

"Are you familiar with the local history?"

"To a large degree. Though my family is considered newcomers—my ancestors arrived about 1860 via the abolitionist underground railway—I grew up hearing the stories of the town's history and its legends."

Tales of ghosts? Emily wondered. "I guess if the town still thinks of you as the new kid on the block, I shouldn't be so upset at the welcome I've been getting, or not getting, after only a couple of weeks."

"You'll find most of the population quite willing to accept you once you've been here awhile." The librarian reshelved a book that had been placed out of order. "The descendants of the original settlers are a bit clannish, however."

"I suspected as much."

"There are perhaps a dozen or two families that were here pre-Revolutionary War. Since then there have been any number of intermarriages. They very much stick to themselves, I'm afraid, and some have been quite successful in business. You'll find their names noted in that book."

Emily flicked through the pages. There were drawings of the community dating from the early years and photographs dating from before the turn of the century.

"In that case, I should find some mention of the original Henderson family," she said. And maybe a Captain Witherspoon.

Ms. Carver's gaze slid from the shelf of books to Emily. "I'm familiar with Henderson House, of course, but do you know, I can't recall the Hendersons as being one of the founding families." She shook her head. "At any rate, have a look at that book, and then there are other, more general accounts of New England history that may interest you."

"Thank you. I appreciate your help."

"That's why I'm here." She turned to retreat up the aisle, then stopped. "When you finish with all of that, we have copies of the local newspaper that go back to its founding around 1900. Perhaps for recent history you'll find those of some value.''

Emily settled down at a study table with the history book and a yellow notepad. Only the occasional rustling of the *New York Times* being read by an elderly gentleman disturbed her concentration. The one other library patron was a college-age student half-hidden behind a huge stack of books.

It didn't take her long to develop a list of Honorville's founding families. It read like a *Who's Who* of the local business owners, with Sheriff Belinger's family thrown in.

But nowhere did she find a single mention of the Henderson family. How could any creditable historian have overlooked her ancestors?

Puzzled, she tapped her pencil eraser on the notepad. Selective memory. That had to be the case. The book read like the original settlers were the most devoted Americans in the entire country, throwing off the oppression of King George single-handedly. According to this account, the young men of Honorville bore arms for the Continental Army. That certainly didn't jibe with Cal's story of Tories behind every tree. Not that the locals would be all that pleased to admit the truth in the twentieth century, she imagined.

There was also no indication in the early chapters of the book that a British officer had ever set foot in Honorville.

An uneasy feeling gnawed at the pit of her stomach. What was the truth? she wondered.

Glancing at her watch, she realized she'd only have time to peruse the local newspaper headlines for the last year or so, and then pick up Becky, her young artist-in-training. The rest of her research would have to wait for another day.

She'd only gone back through six months of the weekly tabloid when a headline caught her eye: WINTER RESORT PROPOSED.

"I'll be darned."

Berrington Real Estate, along with a syndicate of local investors, had been urging a huge recreational development northeast of town, just where Henderson House was located.

Greed, she imagined with a sense of relief, had been around even longer than Honorville. Or ghosts.

"I SAW HER GOING into the library."

"She won't learn anything there."

"Don't be so sure."

He stood up. "I'm going to put an end to this."

"We can't risk—"

"You're the one who took the risk. That man she has working for her could have spotted you."

"He didn't."

"I'm going to stop her."

"How?"

"What you don't know won't hurt me."

"I'm not the one who wants someone to get hurt."

He set his jaw at a grim line. "Neither do I. There are more effective ways to get what we want."

RESTLESS DREAMS TORMENTED Calvert that night.

He stood in a clearing in the woods, a place he knew well. Two women beckoned him. Both were blond, with fair skin and faces that were the same yet different. They spoke not to each other, asking only that he join them.

He woke with a start, his body covered in sweat.

He had not been to that clearing in more than two hundred years. Even now, the memories of the place were too raw to risk such a journey, though it was quite near at hand.

Intuitively, he knew the day would come when he must risk revisiting the site of so many memories.

Chapter Eight

"I'm telling you, every single person who's given me a hard time in this town is involved in that resort development syndicate. That's why they want me out of here. They want my property and Henderson House torn down."

It had taken Emily nearly a week to get back into town and check out her theory at city hall. Now, as she and Cal were scraping the old paint from the side of the house, she was having trouble convincing him of the importance of her discoveries.

"I grant it does sound possible, lass, but why wouldn't that Berrington bloke simply come out with the truth of the matter?"

"Because he knew I'd jack up the price, or simply refuse to sell." Like her Great-Aunt Minerva had, she realized with considerable pride. "And to top it off, he's probably guessed—quite correctly—that I'd fight the development tooth and nail."

Paint chips drifted down past the ladder from where Cal worked. Nursing her battered ego, Emily had made it a point to avoid any potentially intimate moments

with him. In the evenings she'd taken to working alone
in her office and going to bed early. He hadn't objected. Apparently she was the only one who had
missed their cozy evenings by the fire.

He hadn't said anything more about the diary, either, though she'd heard him rummaging through the
attic and other unused rooms in the house at night. Her
only consolation was that he appeared to be as restless
as she.

"The syndicate members," she continued, "are a
cast of characters right out of the local history book.
It's all the founding families. There are three or four
Berringtons involved, a couple of Pierces, everybody's favorite sheriff, plus I don't know how many
others of the clan who are featured prominently in local folklore."

"But you said the plans were discarded."

"I'll bet they've just put them on hold. They're
probably going to try for a special permit at the state
level to get past the environmental flap. That's what the
clerk at city hall suspected." A splinter caught her finger and she sucked at it.

"You should be wearing gloves, lass," he admonished softly.

He was certainly observant. And attentive. She always felt his eyes on her, yet he'd made it clear he was
more into looking than doing anything about it. She
wished he didn't have the power to turn her to warm
jelly at the least little sign of interest. "I'll manage.
Becky took my gloves with her to the carriage house."

"What is she up to?"

"I set up her artist's easel and her paints where she can have a good time without worrying about spills. She calls it her 'homework.' Just like her big brother, she says."

"She's a lovely girl. You've done a good job with both your children."

She felt a swell of pride at his compliment. Her kids would always be the most important thing in her life. "Thank you. The last few years have been ... well, difficult."

"Since your husband died."

"Suddenly finding yourself a widow isn't my idea of fun, with or without children."

"You still miss him."

She glanced up. Silhouetted against rain-heavy clouds, Cal looked very strong and capable in his long-sleeved shirt and jeans. With a pang of guilt, she realized since he'd come into her life she had hardly thought of Ted at all. Perhaps it was simply that enough time had passed to put the grief behind her. But she didn't think that was entirely the case. For all the good it did her.

"Things are better now," she said simply, ignoring the urge to grit her teeth. Frustration was definitely a new—and damned uncomfortable—experience.

Calvert climbed down and moved the ladder a few feet to the right. "How did you lose him?" He probably shouldn't pry into her marriage, but his curiosity about what sort of man she had chosen drove him on. It wasn't jealousy, he told himself sternly. That would not be fair.

"Ted? He was killed in a car accident."

"Ah. I knew those carriages were dangerous."

"In the hands of a speeding driver they're deadly."

"I'm sorry. He was a good husband?" If he had not been, Calvert was prepared to make him answer for his failings in some afterlife.

She smiled as though remembering, and Calvert regretted pursuing the subject.

"We had a good marriage, if that's what you're asking. We were both very serious about our jobs—he was an engineer working on the space program." Her curls shifted over her forehead, and she brushed them away with the back of her hand in a gesture so naturally graceful it made Calvert ache for her again. "I won't say he was the most romantic man in the world, but we did love and respect each other. And he was a good father. A woman shouldn't ask for more than that."

A few bits of silk and lace and a romp in the four-poster would suit her better, he thought, but he said, "He seems a paragon of virtue." A word that had never been used where Calvert was concerned.

Emily sat back on her haunches and drew in a deep breath of cool, moist air. Just as well Cal had finished with the roof. It was sure to rain soon.

In many ways, Ted had been quite admirable. And she had loved him. She was sure of that. But he'd been so serious they'd rarely gone dancing together after their marriage, and seldom sought out times for just themselves once the children had arrived. She remembered several Valentine Days he'd forgotten her, and a couple of birthdays, too. Romance was not a part of his nature.

She wondered what his reaction would have been if she had been more sexually aggressive in their relationship.

Shock, she imagined.

Cal, darn him, wasn't much different.

She inhaled another frustrated breath and caught a new scent. Wood smoke.

"Cal, did we leave the fire going in the fireplace?" she asked.

"Not that I know of."

She stood, brushed some twigs from the back of her jeans, and walked slowly to the end of the house. The odor of smoke seemed to be getting stronger. She felt a prickle of anxiety along the back of her neck. Foolish, she thought. There was probably no cause for alarm. No one in New Hampshire had ever heard of smog, so far as she could tell, and they often burned leaves on the ground.

She turned the corner and her heart lodged in her throat.

"Cal! The carriage house. It's on fire!"

Flames licked at the corner of the building. Ugly black smoke rose in a cloud. "Becky!" she screamed, racing toward the double doors.

She had taken only a few steps when an arm snaked around her waist, hauling her up short.

"You call the authorities. I will see to Becky." When she hesitated a fractional beat, Cal ordered, "Do it!" Then he was gone.

In a few long strides, he was at the doors, yanked them opened and vanished into the darkness inside, calling her daughter's name.

Covering her mouth to prevent another scream, Emily whirled and ran for the house. Cal was right. He was faster and stronger. He had the best chance to save Becky.

Emily's job was to get help here as quickly as possible.

The phone call took only seconds but felt like an eternity. When she came back outside there was no sign of Cal or her child.

Instinct took over as she hooked up a hose and turned the water full blast on the flames. She wouldn't think. Didn't dare. *My baby!*

Nausea threatened and her chest burned with the smoke. Her eyes teared; her vision blurred and shifted with the press of her fear. She fought her way closer to the fire.

She heard a bone-chilling crash. Flames and sparks burst through the open door with a terrifying roar. "Becky! Cal!" She aimed the inadequate stream of water at the new outbreak, biting her lower lip so hard she tasted blood.

Cal would save Becky. He had to. She couldn't lose them both. Not two people she loved.

"I have her, lass. Becky is safe."

At the sound of Cal's breathless voice, Emily dropped the hose and flew to him. She hugged Cal and her child in one all-encompassing embrace, sobbing their names, making no distinction in her relief that they were both alive.

"Easy, luv," he whispered. "We came safely out the back way. You'll be squeezing us to death if you do not let go."

She choked back an anxious laugh. Palming Becky's soot-streaked face, she forced a trembling smile. Then she touched Cal's singed whiskers with the same palsied hand and felt the roughened texture for the first time. He covered her hand with his much larger one, gently bringing her palm to his lips.

"Thank you." The words rasped up her tear-filled throat.

"All in a day's work, luv. Take the child, now, and I will give it a go with the hose."

She lifted Becky into her arms and hugged her tight. "It's no use. The whole building is gone."

"Aye. Most likely. But I will do what I can."

As Cal attacked the fire once again, Becky said, "I was scared, Mommy."

"So was I, sweetheart." *Terrified for you both.*

"Cal saved me."

"I know. He risked his life for you."

Becky buried her face at the crook of Emily's neck. "I love him, Mommy."

"I think I do, too," Emily softly replied.

"THE FIRE WAS *not* an accident." Emily planted her fist on her hip and glared daggers at Sheriff Belinger. A steady drizzle had started almost as soon as the fire was out, but the cold drops on her face did little to cool her temper.

"I want an arson investigation," she demanded. "If you can't arrange that, I'll go to your superior. All the way to the governor, if I have to. My child could have died in there." *And the man I'm falling in love with.*

"I've already called Concord, ma'am. They'll have an investigator up here by afternoon." He glanced at the carriage house that was now little more than a charcoal ruin. Living so far out of town, with wood buildings two hundred years old, there had been little hope the volunteer fire department would arrive in time to save it. "I don't abide suspicious fires any more than you do."

"You don't?"

"No ma'am." He covered his damp hair with his hat. "Seems to me things have gotten out of hand," he grumbled under his breath.

"What do you mean by that, Sheriff?" She caught him by the arm before he could walk away. "You know something, don't you? About the transformer . . . and this fire."

He leveled her a very steady look. "All I know for sure is that fires don't go starting by themselves. And you tell me your little girl wasn't playing with matches."

"She wasn't."

"And that you and that Witherspoon fella didn't see or hear nothin' at all."

"We didn't."

"Then as far as I'm concerned, we got ourselves a mystery."

"One that just maybe has to do with a proposed winter resort area?" she challenged. She might as well get this whole, ugly business out in the open right now. "A development that can't happen unless I sell my land?"

He cocked his head and the tiny blue veins mapping his face stood out. "What do you know about that proposal?"

"Enough to know greed could be a perfectly good motivation for setting a fire."

"Now, Mrs. Morrell, I wouldn't go jumpin' to any conclusions if I was you. That resort idea never got off the ground—"

"It won't, either. You can tell your partners that for me. If I have to hire a twenty-four-hour guard, I'm not going to be run out of town. Do I make myself perfectly clear?"

"Yes, ma'am. I'll pass the word along. But I can guarantee you, that's not what this is all about."

Then what was it all about? she wondered as the sheriff drove away. He'd obviously been surprised she'd uncovered the resort development. But his denial had been equally strong.

Nothing about Honorville made any sense.

When she went inside, she found Cal in the kitchen—cleaning an ancient musket.

Her muscles tensed. "Cal, why are you doing that?"

He rammed a cleaning rod down the bore. "I used to be a fair shot."

"I don't believe in guns."

The angry, determined look in his eyes didn't invite an argument. "I do."

A twenty-four-hour guard. "You'll keep it away from the children?"

"Aye."

BY THE TIME PETE ARRIVED home from school, the arson investigator had made his way through the rain-soaked debris of the carriage house, shifting and poking at the muddy mess.

"Looks like this was the problem." The fireman pointed his stick at a fire-blackened metal box. "Electrical fire started here in the circuit box. Overload, I imagine. Smoldered awhile and then ignited. Happens all the time with these old places that were wired in the thirties and forties."

"You mean it wasn't arson?" Emily asked.

The fireman pulled up the collar of his yellow rain slicker. "Doesn't look like it to me. My guess is that woodchucks or rats ate away at the insulation, and when you turned the lights on inside and left them for a time, they heated up. It's not a new story. Just wish folks would check their wiring more often."

Her stomach churned with guilt at the thought she'd actually sent Becky out here to play so she wouldn't make a mess in the house. Talk about shortsighted. "I promise you, there'll be an electrician out here as soon as I can get one."

He tipped his hat. "Good idea. The main house was probably wired at the same time. This far out of town, I'd advise a sprinkler system, too."

As the fireman left, Cal said, "It seems with each new invention there are also dangers." He looped his arm around her shoulder in a protective gesture.

Instinctively, she leaned into his strength. "I was so sure...."

"In this case, it is better to have been wrong."

"I suppose." Cal's shirt still smelled of smoke. She shivered at the thought that both he and her daughter might have been killed in the fire. "Whatever the cause of the fire, the net result is still a blow to my profit-and-loss projections. I'd counted on the extra accommodations to—"

"Don't think about it now, luv. It is time we get you in out of the cold. Looks like winter is on the way." Rain dampened his dark hair with diamond drops that she wanted desperately to smooth away with her hand.

She swallowed the lump in her throat and fought back a new wave of emotion that welled up inside her. "Are you going to put your musket away?"

He squeezed her gently. "Not just yet."

CAL'S TEACUP CLATTERED onto the kitchen counter, spilling the contents. He grabbed a cloth to clean up the mess, and the material bit into his palm.

"Something wrong?" Emily asked from across the room.

"No." He flexed the fingers of his right hand.

She frowned. "Are you hurt?"

"It is nothing, lass."

"Let me see."

"Do not trouble yourself."

She took his hand and examined the palm. A nasty red welt extended across the width. "Cal, you've been burned. Why didn't you say something?"

"Because—"

"You men all think you have to be macho. You go for hours in pain just so you can be a tough guy. Wait right here," she ordered. "I've got some salve that will help."

Cal stared down at his hand in disbelief. The wound stung like bloody hell. It had all afternoon. Which was ridiculous. Ghosts didn't get hurt. It was simply not possible. Yet it had even bothered him during dinner and when he had carried Becky up the stairs to tuck her into bed for the night.

Quite a puzzling development.

Emily returned with a tube of lotion and took his hand once again, smoothing the ointment across his palm. He noted the subtle differences in texture between his hand and hers, fair on dark, delicate against the broad expanse of his palm. As she bent over him, the light caught her hair. Not a solid color at close inspection, it was alive with every conceivable shade of gold and silver, light and shadow, and carried her intoxicating citrus scent.

Desire knotted his muscles, and he failed to stifle a groan.

"I'm sorry," she said. "I didn't mean to hurt you."

As she looked up, Calvert indulged himself by letting his gaze caress her cheekbones and finely sculpted lips, the sweet blueness of her eyes. "You caused me no pain," he said, his voice hoarse. His agony was self-inflicted, centered deep in his groin and curling out in heated phalanxes to attack him from all sides. "'Tis only that I wish I were a painter so I could capture your beauty and keep it always with me."

The shake of her head belied the pleasure in her eyes. "I bet you use that line with all the girls." Her light laughter seemed strained.

"Nay. You are the first." It was true. At this moment he could scarcely remember any other woman.

"Cal, I..." She glanced away as though she could not speak the words that had come to her lips. Taking up a strip of gauze, she wrapped it loosely around his wound, then lifted her gaze to his again. "I guess...there's really no way I can properly thank you for saving Becky."

"There is no need, my dear."

"I know it's inadequate, but..." She reached up and, as innocently as a young girl, placed a feather-light kiss on his lips.

The unexpected sensation jolted him. Like a musket shot at close range, it reverberated in his head and through the length of his bones. It was the briefest of connections, but it staggered him. And he wanted more. God help him, he *had* to fully taste this woman. Once.

Though he knew deep in his gut once would never be enough, he lowered his head to hers.

Emily watched in amazement as myriad emotions crossed Cal's rugged features. Shock no greater than her own. Surprise mixed with pleasure. And finally—dared she hope—hungry desire that matched the riotous feelings her brief kiss had conjured deep within her.

His indigo eyes trapped her as surely as though he'd run her through with his sword, pinning her to the wall. And her heart ached with the same painful intensity. *Kiss me back,* she silently pleaded as his head inched toward hers. *Before my pride makes me turn away once again.*

His hand teased near her face, touching her hair so lightly she imagined the sensation more than felt it, as if he were afraid the strands were too fragile to withstand a more violent onslaught. *Not so,* she responded internally. I won't break if you kiss me, hold me, love me.

Lethargy crept into her limbs. She could neither stand her ground nor flee, so great was the need that threatened her equilibrium.

"Are you all right, lass?"

She nodded, aware of the husky timbre of his voice and how her hands had slipped to his upper arms, her fingers digging into his muscles. Her brain had gone into slow motion. Lack of oxygen, she mused, convinced all the blood had flowed from her head to settle and throb at a much lower elevation, leaving her dizzy and disoriented.

The first tentative brush of his lips sent her off on a whirlwind trip. She spun out of control. All logic fled; only feeling remained. Warm. So colorful it was slashed with primary shades of eloquence. Sensual beyond belief.

When he forcefully deepened the kiss, she discovered he tasted of sweet English tea and hot, vibrant passion. She relished the experience, each thrust of his tongue, every shifting of his moist mouth on hers, the scraping of his whiskers across her sensitive skin. The radiating pleasure, more exciting than she had ever known, caused her to tremble and her breathing to quicken in short, raspy sounds.

Calvert heard her soft moan of pleasure, and the sound drove him on. He slipped his hand to the swell of her hips, pressing her against the hard ridge of his arousal. Sweet ecstasy. She was so passionate, so irresistible that the longing within him was a sharp blade of need.

Yet he suspected, at some deep, intuitive level, that her response was in part that of a woman who had been without a man for too long. It made him heartsick. That, and the knowledge that he could not assuage her need. Ghosts, he was quite confident, did not have the capacity. Yet the urge he felt . . . the painful ache . . .

None of that mattered.

"Ah, luv, we can't do this," he whispered against her sweet lips in an agony far worse than hanging. "There's no future, you see."

Emily went rigid. "I'm not asking for commitment."

"It's more than that, luv. It is simply that as a ghost, I cannot—"

She turned and snatched up the first-aid kit and tube of ointment. "I've had it with you and that damned ghost story of yours. If you don't want me, I can deal with that. But I'm sick to death of the mixed messages you're sending out. Every time I think something wonderful is going to happen, you back off." She slammed the lid shut on the case. "Either you tell me the truth or you're going to get out of my house. Stick *that* in your ghost story!" Her stomach churned and her hands shook.

"Dearest Emily—"

"Don't give me any more of your silver tongue. Or your cockamamy stories. You're no more a ghost than I am."

"But I am."

She shot him a withering look. "Oh, yeah? When was the last time you heard about a ghost who burned his hand?"

He glanced at the offending limb. "It is a bit perplexing."

"You're damn right it is. And unless I've forgotten my sex education classes, a moment ago you were fully aroused. Like ready, buster. And so was I." She let the tension drift out of her shoulders. "And I'm not easy, Cal. Whatever you may think, that's not the case."

"I never considered—"

"Then what's the problem, Cal? What the hell is going on between us? What's it all about?"

Chapter Nine

"Ah, lass, if I understood it myself, I would be happy to explain."

"Try. Please. You're driving me crazy, Cal."

"More than once since it all happened, I, too, have questioned my sanity." He lifted one lean hip and settled it on the edge of the maple table. "It is not a thing easily believed."

Emily twisted her lips in a wry smile. "I can imagine."

"Particularly by a skeptic who does not believe in ghosts."

A blast of wind shook the kitchen window and angry drops of rain splattered against the glass. The storm had finally arrived in full force.

"Convince me." She leaned back against the counter and folded her arms across her chest. Her breasts were still incredibly sensitive, aching with unfulfilled passion. Damn him for doing his backpedaling number to her again…and her, for allowing her good sense to be overridden by sexual attraction, plus other emotions she wasn't prepared to name again so soon.

He rubbed his palm across his chin, and she remembered the erotic feel of his whiskers brushing against her flesh. She gritted her teeth.

"It was after I was hung, you see. The pain was a biting thing, but soon in passing. Then I was in darkness so black it was like being in a cave without a flame to guide me. I was floating. Quite without weight and having no sense of up or down, right or left. Not an unpleasant sensation but rather a disquieting one."

"The astronauts enjoy it," she mumbled.

He raised a questioning eyebrow.

"Never mind. Go on."

"Then I discovered a light. Very bright. Like a thousand torches beckoning me onward. A part of me wanted to float in that direction. Out of the darkness. But I resisted."

Outside, a wind-driven branch scraped against the side of the house. She shivered and hugged herself more closely.

"It sounds to me you had a near-death out-of-body experience. There's been a lot written on the subject . . ." Which, she realized, he could have read anywhere, at least in this century. ". . . though I don't necessarily believe—"

"I speak only the truth, dear Emily." He slid his bandaged hand along his thigh, and she envied the denim fabric that could feel his caress while she could not. "When I stubbornly resisted the invitation of the light, I apparently attracted their attention."

"Their?"

"They did not give themselves a name, though over the years I have come to think of them as the Keepers of the black tunnel and the light."

His imagination had certainly gone into high gear, she thought. As had hers. With the storm churning outside and the kitchen curtain fluttering in a cold draft of air, it was almost easy to believe in ghosts and goblins. But she wasn't willing to concede just yet. "These Keepers of yours. Did you actually talk to them?"

He paused thoughtfully. "I never truly heard the sound of voices, theirs or mine, yet we did communicate. I know not how."

A ghost who dabbled in mental telepathy or mind reading on the side? It figured, she thought with a weary sigh. "And just what did you and these Keepers discuss?"

"That I had been unfairly hung and deserved the right to clear my name before I went with them. I was quite adamant. I simply would not go forward as they wished me to. Dug in my heels, as they say."

Emily felt like digging a hole and throwing Cal in. His whole story was just this side of ludicrous. He was either the smoothest liar on earth or he truly believed his tale.

"The discussion went on at considerable length, as I recall, though judging time under the circumstances was, of course, difficult. When the light began to fade, I knew I was wearing out their patience."

"You have a tendency to do that very well." Hers was near the breaking point. Her nerves had never felt so jangled, or her sexual tension so high. If only he'd just forget all this ghost business and make love to her....

"Yes. I have been known to make life difficult for others when I make up my mind to the task. I remember well the time a merchant provided my father with shoddy merchandise. I searched him out—"

"Cal, stick to the subject."

"Yes, of course." One of his charming smiles lifted his lips, and Emily blew out an exasperated sigh. "When I felt the Keepers' resolve weakening, I vowed to them I would return after I found Alice's diary and cleared the Witherspoon name. I owed that to my father, you see."

"You mean you promised to toddle on back to their tunnel and *die* if they let you go in search of the diary?"

"Aye. As a gentleman and an officer in His Majesty's Own, I gave my word of honor. My good name is the only thing I have ever had of value. And therein, dear Emily, lies my dilemma."

Her dilemma was one of weighing the facts as she knew them, as she had felt them in Cal's arms and understood them with her rational mind, versus buying into his story. "Where does all this leave me...us?"

He shoved away from the table. Taking her gently by the shoulders, he said, "Do you not see? Even if I could—we could—be lovers, once I find the diary I would have to leave you. I gave my word." There was a look of deep sadness and regret in his eyes.

"You've been looking for two hundred years." *Couldn't you squeeze me into your schedule for a night or two?*

"But I will find it, luv. Since you have arrived I have somehow felt closer to the diary than ever before. As if Alice were trying to send a message through you."

"I didn't arrive in Honorville special delivery, Cal, from this world or the next. And at the rate you've been going, my grandchildren could be dead and buried before the diary turns up." And she'd be nothing but dried bones. Frustrated ones at that.

"It's no use, luv. A man's oath is the best he can give."

She placed her hands on his chest. Remembering how its breadth was furred with dark hair, she regretted she'd never be able to explore the springy curls.

Lifting her chin, she said, "If that's how you feel, Cal, then I guess there's nothing left for us to say." Or do.

"I'm sorry, lass. Truly I am."

So was she.

The rain pelted down outside, but with no more fury than the tears she refused to shed.

CALVERT PACED THE FLOOR most of the night. His word. His honor. What did they mean in the face of what he felt for Emily?

It was like his soul was being ripped apart.

What could he offer her? *Nothing*, came the response from deep in his gut.

She deserved so much more.

The argument raged until he couldn't sleep or think.

He shook his fist at the unseen, unhearing Keepers. The only reply was silence. Why had he promised so much?

His ruminations took him to the basement, out of hearing of those above, and he tore the space apart searching for the diary. Dust stung his nostrils and filled his lungs.

"Alice! Alice!" he cried. "Why did you betray me?" And what should I do with the woman who so distantly has sprung from your loins? A woman as loving as you.

THE FOLLOWING MORNING, Pete had just left to catch the school bus when Emily heard the doorbell. Thinking her son might have forgotten something and found the door locked, she hurried to see what was the matter.

A slender young man dressed in a business suit and raincoat stood on her front porch. His rain-spattered glasses were dwarfed by his huge, beaked nose.

"Mrs. Morrell?" he asked.

"Yes. What can I do for you?"

"Leroy Abernathy, ma'am, from the county's Business Licensing Bureau."

She wished everyone under thirty hadn't suddenly started calling her "ma'am." It made her feel like she'd slipped over the hill without even being aware she'd made it to the top. Cal's rejection of the night before didn't help matters. "Is there a problem?" She opened the door wider.

He slapped the rain from his hat and stepped inside. "Yes, ma'am. It's about you not having a license to run a rooming house."

"There must be some mistake. I plan to turn this into a bed and breakfast when I'm ready to accept guests, but I was told I'd have no trouble getting permits when the time came." She'd checked out zoning requirements quite carefully.

"You wouldn't have had any trouble getting a license, ma'am, if you had applied and brought the building up to code. But we've been told that you already have a boarder."

"Boarder?" Was he talking about Cal?

"Yes, ma'am. And that means you're out of compliance and there'll have to be a pretty substantial fine—"

"Now wait a minute . . ."

Upstairs, Calvert softly closed the door to his room. He'd heard the doorbell and had stood listening to the caller long enough to get the gist of the conversation. What he'd heard, he didn't like.

It looked like Emily's enemies were still determined to frighten her off. Stuff and nonsense, the way government tried to run a body's business. He thought the colonists had gotten rid of all that. Wasn't that what the rebellion had been all about?

He quickly changed out of his work clothes and donned his uniform. Picking up his musket, he tried to walk through the door without bothering to open it, just as he had for the last two hundred years.

The door smacked him right in the face, knocking his hat off.

"*Damnation!*" What the devil was going on?

Tentatively, he touched the door, trying to shove his hand through the solid walnut panel.

The door remained unyielding.

What plague had suddenly struck that he couldn't perform a simple feat like walking through a closed door? Any honest-to-goodness ghost worth his salt could do that.

But Calvert couldn't. When he tried the wall, he found it just as impervious to his efforts as the door had been.

"Hell and damnation!"

In disgust, he yanked open the door and marched down the stairs. He couldn't even seem to make himself invisible.

Emily heard Cal coming but continued to argue with the young man from the license bureau. "Surely there's an appeals process. Someone I can talk to."

"It won't do you any good, ma'am. The source of our information is quite—" He halted his thought in midsentence. His eyes grew as round as the glasses perched on his nose.

She flicked a glance behind her and almost choked to find Cal glowering at the young man from the stairway. He was in full dress regalia, sword at his hip and musket cradled in his arms. She forced herself to keep a straight face. She knew just what Cal was up to and it tickled her funny bone.

"What were you saying, Mr. Abernathy?" she asked innocently.

He swallowed visibly. "Your boarder..." He pointed with a trembling finger. "That man..."

She turned slowly. Cal was indeed a frightening sight, if one was unprepared. "What man is that? I see no one."

"But there...on the stairs..." The poor man was white as a sheet.

"Oh, my." She tossed off his fear with a flick of her hand. "Has that ol' Henderson ghost shown up again? He does pop up at the oddest moments." She laughed lightly, as though having a resident ghost was the most common thing in the world. Which, in her case, it was. "Now surely the county is not saying I have to have a license to have my house haunted?"

"No, ma'am. There're no ordinances about..." He shoved his glasses higher up on his nose. "You can't see him?"

Turning to look at the stairs, she said, "I certainly don't see anything out of the ordinary." Not for her house.

The young man backed up to the door. "You're sure?" His voice cracked.

"Absolutely. Are you feeling all right, Mr. Abernathy? You're looking just a bit pale. You mustn't let a ghost—"

She heard the metal clank of the bolt on the musket and pictured Cal pointing his long weapon at the youthful bureaucrat.

With a choked cry and a panicky look, the young man turned and fled out the door.

Emily covered her mouth with her hand so she wouldn't laugh out loud. Her body shook; her ribs ached.

"Oh, Cal." She laughed when she heard the man's car spin up a shower of gravel on the driveway and race away from the house. "You were wonderful." She turned and smiled at him. Her heart constricted painfully at the sight of how very handsome he looked in his military attire. So imposing. Thoroughly masculine. And she didn't dare tell him so, or acknowledge even to herself how much she still wanted him in spite of the stories he'd told. Or his decision to not take advantage of her willingness. *Foolishness,* she mentally amended.

"I was jolly good, wasn't I?" he agreed smugly, resting the butt of the musket on the entryway floor.

"You can bet it will be a long time before any county inspector comes out here to harass me again. I've never heard of such a ridiculous thing. Needing a license to have one guest in the house."

"Yes, truly a ridiculous idea." The smile faded from his face. "Emily, I believe something has gone amiss with me."

Worried, she touched his arm. "What is it, Cal? Are you sick?"

He shook his head. "Though it does not in the least seem possible, I find I can no longer walk through walls."

Thank goodness. Maybe there was a chance he'd come to his senses and they'd get to the bottom of this ghost nonsense. "It's all right. I'm sure things will sort themselves out. Be brave."

"I fear cowardice is more my style."

"Don't be silly."

"'Tis true. You need only ask my military superiors. They will assure you—"

"If they could hang you by mistake then I see no reason to take their word for you being a coward."

"But you see, there was an unfortunate incident near Boston. I had a group of lads with me. Six in all. We were surveying the neighborhood when we blundered on a company of Continentals. A navigation error on their part, I assure you, as they were well away from where they ought to have been."

"What happened?" Emily suspected Cal would be the best storytelling innkeeper in the state if given a chance. She loved to hear his voice, his cultured British accent and the mellow tones that settled across her flesh like warm velvet.

"They spotted us. Dreadful. We had no chance. None at all." He shrugged. "So I told the lads to run like the devil himself was on their tail—which was very nearly the truth, seeing that the odds were a hundred to our six."

"I don't call that cowardly. It sounds pretty darned intelligent to me."

"My superiors did not see it in quite the same light." He lifted his musket and cradled it in his arms again. "When I told the lads to run, I stayed behind to let fire a couple of shots to keep the rebels at bay. Then I followed after my men. The injury I received—"

"You were wounded?" Her heart twisted with concern.

He rubbed at his buttocks. "Aye, a coward's wound, they said. Not serious but bloody embarrassing, I assure you."

Keeping a straight face wasn't easy. "Cal, you're as brave a man as I have ever known. Just yesterday you ran into a burning building to save my daughter's life."

"That was not bravery, lass. I had nothing to lose."

"Because you're a ghost?" She shook her head. That same lame excuse that had her gritting her teeth for more reasons than one. "Did you think about being a ghost when you ran into the carriage house? Or did you simply act on instinct because you care about Becky?"

With a puzzled look, he considered her question. "Only because of the child."

"You see? In my book, that's what bravery is all about." Among both ghosts and humans, she suspected, not that she believed in the former. Most of the time.

Calvert wasn't entirely convinced, but he couldn't resist the impulse her words had triggered, an urge he seemed quite unable to resist. He lowered his musket to his side again, then cupped her chin in his hand.

Her eyes questioned him, darkening a shade in anticipation. The delicate seam of her lips separated for the same reason. Slowly, he crossed her mouth with his.

Sweet heaven! The taste of ambrosia. The power of Emily's distinctive elixir gripped him like a powerful aphrodisiac. Need ripped through him.

Though they touched only where their lips met and his hand caressed her cheek, he felt the leap of her heart along his whole body. His thighs were hot, stomach muscles taut, groin aching. *None* of that should be happening. Not to a ghost.

"Aw, lass, what are you doing to me?" His voice was thick with frustration.

"I thought you were doing it to me." The tip of her tongue slid along the edge of her lower lip and muscles tightened once again in Calvert's gut.

"I would like to have you here, now, this very moment, and would if I could."

Her eyes widened. "In the hallway?"

"Aye. Does that thought excite you, lass?" It did Calvert, though it should not be true. The throw rug, with its paisley swirls of gold and red, would do nicely for a mattress and provide a fine backdrop for Emily's creamy, white flesh.

"I've never . . ." She placed a trembling hand on his wrist. "Becky's in the kitchen. We can't—"

"'Tis not possible. I know that better than you." And it would surely be a disastrous mistake to try after all these years.

He kissed her softly, savoring all too briefly the sweetness of her nectar. He needed to gain some distance from this woman, to study his problem. If not, surely he would not be responsible for his actions.

"Emily, my dear, would you consider . . . that is, if I could have a bit of my wages . . ."

"You're going somewhere?" A look of puzzled hurt shadowed her lovely eyes.

"A day off, perhaps. Nothing more."

Emily lifted her chin against the sudden, tight feeling in her chest. "Of course. You've worked hard. You deserve that." If he was going to leave her, she wouldn't try to stop him.

By the time she found her purse and returned with what little cash she had on hand, Cal had already changed back into his jeans and flannel shirt. He met her in the hallway.

She forced herself to ask the one question she needed answered. "Cal, are you planning to come back?" Thankfully, her voice had remained steady.

"Aye, lass." His lips tilted into a smile. "You will not be getting rid of me so easily."

Relief washed over her and she exhaled the breath she hadn't realized she'd been holding.

Emily stood rooted in place as Cal walked out the front door. He was the most disturbing, unpredictable . . . He'd wanted for one minute to make love with her in the hallway. Lord, if she could have gotten him to act on his softly couched threat, by damn, she'd have done it!

Then he'd simply walked out the door.

The now familiar weight of frustration settled around her.

It wasn't often Emily gave up on anything she wanted. Cal was beginning to look like the exception that made the rule. *A ghost, my foot!* He'd come running to her rescue when that stupid bureaucrat had shown up at her door. Cal's kisses were decidedly real—for both of them. She'd felt his hunger. It wasn't as if he didn't care about her.

Then why the hell—

She glanced outside to see Cal rounding the corner onto the road. A little smile tugged at the corners of her lips.

"I don't understand you, Calvert T. Witherspoon, but I know damn well you feel something for me. Maybe you aren't willing to admit it now. But you will. Count on it."

"YOUR PLAN DIDN'T WORK very well."

"Poor Leroy had to go home sick. He'll be in bed for a week."

"She's clever."

"Smarter than you are. You could have really botched things up with the fire. The little girl—"

"That wasn't my doing."

"If there is any evidence—"

"There won't be."

The room grew silent. Someone poured a cup of coffee, and the pot clattered back onto the stove.

"We're going to have to think of another way."

"What?"

"I don't know." Desperation laced her words.

"One of us will have to make a sacrifice."

"Who?"

A dozen pair of eyes turned toward one man in the room.

"YOU LOOK LIKE A MAN with a problem." The burly barkeep had a neck as thick as most men's thighs. He placed a second glass of ale in front of Calvert and gave the mahogany counter a swipe with his rag.

"Aye. 'Tis true. I have walked the countryside most of the day and still no answers have come to me."

"Must be woman trouble."

"In part," Calvert conceded, though not the usual sort. He was quite accomplished at handling those.

The pub was a quiet one with few customers passing through while he had been sipping the tasteless brew.

"I solved my problem by dumping my old lady," the barkeep said.

Calvert frowned. "'Tis not an *old* lady who concerns me. Nor do I wish to *dump* her, whatever that might entail."

Shrugging, the bear of a man said, "We all got troubles, buddy. Just look at me. Been runnin' this place for the last ten years. Now the damn town council has some kinda bee up their rear. Don't want to renew my license. Hell, there's never been no trouble here to speak of."

"It seems the government is always trying to interfere in an honest day's work." As they had that morning with Emily.

"It's that mayor we've got. Pierce. He owns the drugstore just down the block. Nothin' happens in this town without his say-so. I heard one of his buddies wants to open up a bar and restaurant the other end of town. He don't want no competition."

"I see." Calvert drummed his fingers on the counter. Perhaps that explained Emily's problems, as well. Though it seemed to him that, being so far out of town, Henderson House would provide little competition for the inns in town.

"I had to ask my cousin to do an end run for me. He's married to some gal who's a niece or somethin' to one of these local mucky-mucks who think they own the whole damn town."

"Ah, yes, connections are always valuable." And Emily, he realized, had none, just as his family had done poorly in running the gauntlet of tawdry politics with the Crown. "Do you, by chance, know a bloke named Berrington?"

The man tidied the napkins in their holder. "Sure. He's one of 'em. He took his father's place on the town council when the old man died a couple of years back."

The barkeep moved down the counter to serve a newly arrived customer. Calvert continued to drink, though there seemed few ready answers to his multiple problems in the poor imitation of ale he had been served.

THE HEADLIGHTS OF A CAR in the driveway flashed across the living room windows. Emily resisted the urge to run to the front door. It was well after two in the morning.

She'd vacillated all day between worry and anger, finally dozing on the couch because she couldn't bring herself to go to bed until Cal reappeared. If he ever did.

The doorknob rattled.

She frowned. She'd intentionally left the door unlocked. Why didn't he come on in? And who, she wondered, had brought Cal home?

Then she heard him singing…at the top of his lungs. The bawdy song reverberated in the country silence.

Good lord! The man was drunk.

She raced to the door, threw it open and found Cal grinning at her in a way that made her heart do a quick little two-step. The man was impossible. Even so, she felt a surge of relief that he was home safely.

Bowing, he swept off an imaginary hat. "Mistress Morrell, I fear I am in my cups."

"You certainly are." He smelled like a brewery. Repressing a smile, she said, "Come on in. Let's get you up to bed before you wake the whole neighborhood."

"The barkeep was kind enough to see me home in his carriage."

"Very thoughtful of him." She hooked her hand through his arm.

For a moment he stood in the hallway, wavering a little as he looked up to the second-floor landing. "I see you have added a new stairway in my absence. I quite agree two stairways make for a nice balance."

"Let's take the one on the right, shall we?" The man was so pie-eyed, he was seeing double. At least he was a happy drunk. "Come on. One foot after the other. Up we go."

She managed to get him to his bedroom where he collapsed his length on the narrow bed.

"Come on, Cal. You can't sleep like that. You've got to get your clothes off."

He managed to roll onto his side and pat the bed beside him, staring at her with blurry eyes. "There's room for two, lass. Shall we give it a go?"

Not tonight. Now if he'd been serious about this morning's invitation... "I'll take a rain check, thanks." She pulled off one of his boots and dropped it to the floor.

"Is it raining? I paid scant attention."

He probably wouldn't have noticed a tornado. "I just don't think you're up to much of anything tonight."

Looking offended, he said, "I assure you, I have received few complaints from the ladies."

This one had a major complaint about his lousy timing.

After considerable tugging, the second boot joined the first on the floor. "Off with your shirt and pants, mister," she ordered.

"Quite right. I've always enjoyed a lass who knew what she was about." His quirky grin was a pale imitation of a sexy leer. He fumbled with the buttons on his shirt.

This wasn't going well, and Emily was reluctant to get too intimately involved in the undressing process. Cal might be drunk. She was stone-cold sober and acutely aware they were in his bedroom. While his bed was narrow, the temptation to cuddle with him for just a few minutes, even if that was all that would happen, was pretty damn inviting. She'd like to spoon her back against his chest and match the bend of his knees with hers. If his hand drifted a bit to cup her breasts, she wouldn't mind. Maybe in the morning when he woke up he'd be feeling better. Then . . .

Blowing out a frustrated sigh, Emily hauled the quilt out from under Cal and spread it across him. "I guess you can survive one night sleeping in your clothes."

As she tried to tuck the down-filled comforter around his shoulders, he caught her by the wrist. He met her gaze, his eyes suddenly clear and very sober.

"I am sorry, Em," he said, his voice a hoarse whisper.

She wasn't quite sure what he was sorry about. Before she had a chance to ask, his eyes had drooped shut and he was snoring softly.

Combing back the lock of hair that had fallen across his forehead, she sighed again. "I'm sorry, too." Going to bed with Cal was just what she wanted, she admitted, but not when he was drunk. She wondered if she'd ever get a better invitation than the one she just turned down.

She studied the well-shaped curve of his dark eyebrows and the fan of his long lashes brushing his ruddy cheeks. He had good bone structure. Very masculine and quite compelling. As were his lips.

Dipping her head, she pressed a soft kiss to his warm lips. "Sleep tight, Calvert T. Witherspoon. Ask me again when you're sober."

IN THE MORNING, Cal's eyes were red-rimmed. Emily handed him two aspirins and a glass of tomato juice laced with Worcestershire sauce. "Maybe these will help," she said.

He gulped the pills down. "It seems I underestimated the potency of the local brew."

"It can sneak up on you, I'm sure."

He eased himself into a chair at the table. "Most especially when it has been so long between drinks. I think the next time will be even longer." Leaning his elbow on the table, he rubbed his head with his hand.

"That's a good idea." She touched him gently on the shoulder. There wasn't much you could do about a hangover except wait it out. "When you were gone all day yesterday, it started me thinking. I know I have a problem getting too absorbed in my work and forgetting everything else. It seems to me we ought to plan at least one day off each week. Maybe do something special." As a family—you and me and the children.

"Trying to keep me sober, are you, lass?" He cocked a crooked eyebrow.

"No." I'm trying to make you see just how much you care about me.

"I trust... About last night. I hope I did not do anything that... I have little recollection—"

"You were a perfect gentleman." More or less, to Emily's everlasting regret.

Chapter Ten

Overall, it had been a most pleasant day, Calvert decided, holding the door open as Emily and the youngsters preceded him out of the diner. On their way home from a Saturday matinee, they had stopped at a small, greasy-smelling restaurant in Honorville for the children's favorite hamburgers. As they headed for the car, Brady Berrington hurried toward them.

Calvert stifled an oath. It *had* been a pleasant day.

"Emily! I'm glad I spotted your car," Brady said.

"Why? Is there something wrong?"

Calvert hung back a few paces. He did not like the man, and felt sure that he, along with others who held political power, were at the crux of Emily's troubles. He wanted to be ready for any emergency. Pity he'd left his sabre at home.

"No, no. Nothing like that," Brady insisted. "It's just that I dropped by your house today and no one was at home."

"We went to Concord for a matinee." Emily rested her hand on Becky's shoulder. "What was it you wanted?"

"Well, I..." He looked at the child and then back at Emily. "I wonder if I might have a word with you in private?"

"If it's about selling the house, Brady, you already know how I feel."

"It's not that. Really. It's just a bit personal."

Calvert noticed the man's nervousness, the way he swallowed every few moments, and he didn't like it at all. What was the bloke up to now? he wondered.

"I'm sure anything you have to say can be said in front of my children," Emily indicated. "I rarely keep secrets from them."

Peter had already reached the car. "Hey, mom," he shouted, "are we going, or what?"

"In a minute, dear."

"Well, you see, Emily, I've been thinking." Brady's Adam's apple fluttered up and down like a puppet on a string. "You know I'm a bachelor. Never married."

"No, I didn't know that," Emily replied, her expression puzzled.

"Well, you see, I know of this rather nice restaurant in Concord. Continental cuisine. I thought perhaps...you and I, that is..."

Dark rage twisted through Calvert. The bloody sod was actually trying to court *his* woman. Of all the gall!

His hands balling into fists, he watched their conversation. The man was all harsh angles and planes, in contrast to Emily's soft, feminine curves. Today she had worn a skirt—he had hoped it was for him—that fell in gentle folds across her lush hips. Her blouse was of a fabric that clung much like silk, shifting with a soft, sibilant sound each time she moved.

In the darkness of the theater he had been aware of her, her scent, her restlessness, and his ache to hold her against all threats that might come her way.

He longed for the sweet feel of her body pressed against his, the taste of her lips, the agony of denial. Possessiveness ripped through him like a razor-sharp knife polished to a high sheen.

Now some other blighter held her attention.

Not that she was doing anything wrong, he admitted with a grim set to his jaw. She was simply talking to the man. Barely even a smile on her lips. Though there was, he noticed, high color on her cheeks.

But he was too angry to care.

It should be he, Calvert T. Witherspoon, who was inviting her to dine, not in a greasy restaurant where she paid the bill, but at some elegant establishment with lush velvet chairs and private booths where a man and a woman could... Just the kind of place where Berrington no doubt intended to seduce—

He took two steps forward. His hand futilely sought his weapon. With a jolt, he recalled another Berrington, one of the spies he had recruited for the Crown. He hadn't much liked that fellow, either.

"I imagine I'm supposed to be flattered you asked, Brady," she said, "but I really can't go out with you. It just wouldn't be right." Becky scurried off to join her brother at the car.

"May I ask why not?" Brady seemed quite taken aback.

"You underestimate my intelligence, Mr. Berrington. Ever since I arrived, you and your cronies have been trying to drive me out of my house. I don't know why, but you can bet your gas-guzzling Cadillac I'm going to find out."

He sputtered. "Emily, my dear, I had only hoped to— My intentions are quite honorable, I assure you. Matrimony is—"

"Excuse me. My children are waiting." She stalked past the man to her car.

Calvert wanted to let out a whoop of celebration but restrained himself. Giving Berrington a withering look, he followed Emily to the car.

"Good girl, lass. You told him a thing or two."

She glared at him across the top of the car. "What business is it of yours if a man asks me out or not?"

"Well, none, I suppose, but—"

"You're darn right it's not."

She climbed into the car, and Calvert took his place on the passenger side. The children had already settled themselves in the back seat. "I had only hoped—"

"What is it with you?" she asked, shoving the key forcefully into the steering column. "You've made it abundantly clear you're not interested in me."

"That's not true, luv. You know I cannot—"

Her head whipped around and she nailed him with a look that rocked him. "Calvert, you are absolutely green with jealousy."

"Not so," he denied, knowing it was a lie.

She sighed and leaned her head back on the bolster. The guy was driving her crazy, and having Brady ask her out made matters worse. She didn't *want* to go out with anybody. She wanted, darn it all, to go to *bed* with Cal.

"Let me see if I've got this right," she said, speaking softly so the children wouldn't hear. "You keep insisting you're a ghost."

"Aye."

"When, Captain Witherspoon, have you ever heard of a ghost who was jealous for no reason at all, got his hand burned doing something very brave, can't walk through walls, and gets drunk as a skunk? Tell me that, will you?" And I'll check myself into the local psychiatric hospital, she thought, twisting the ignition key.

He covered her hand. "All I know, lass, is if that Berrington bloke with his beady eyes ever touches you, I'll throttle him with my bare hands, if need be, and damn the consequences. A man can only be hung once."

She smiled and laughed a low sound, her tension draining away. The battle she was fighting was an impossible one to win. "I don't think I'll ever understand you, Cal... but thank you for caring."

Emily signaled and wheeled the car out into traffic, wondering why on earth she loved him so much. It wasn't at all logical. But then, perhaps hearts were not a part of the anatomy that responded to rational thinking.

She also couldn't understand what Brady had been up to by trying to date her. *Matrimony?* The mere thought turned her stomach and made little sense from Brady's point of view. Unless he believed she was so desperate for a man she'd succumb to both his advances and then his urgings to sell her house.

Not in this lifetime, she thought, her hands closing more tightly around the steering wheel.

A FEW DAYS LATER, Emily sought escape from the persistent tension that sizzled between her and Cal. With each day that passed, she wanted him more, not less, and was appalled by her total lack of self-discipline. Solving logic problems had never been so engrossing.

Either the guy had the self-restraint of a saint, or she had really lost her touch.

She left Becky in his care and headed to the library to do more research about the founders of Honorville, and their descendants.

The first large drops of a new, and very chilly, storm pelted her windshield as she pulled into the library parking lot.

"I'm so glad you dropped by again." Irene Carver smiled up at Emily from behind her desk. "Among other things, I wanted to tell you how sorry I was about your fire."

"I'm just glad no one was hurt. Though the loss doesn't exactly help my budget projections for the business."

"I imagine that's true." The librarian's soft voice was filled with sympathy. "At any rate, the last time you came by, when you mentioned the Henderson family as town founders, it piqued my interest. It seemed like an interesting oversight in our local history books."

"I find it strange, too." Emily slipped off her warm jacket and held it in her arms. After the cold air outside, the library seemed overheated.

"I contacted the university library. They sent me a copy of a master's thesis on New Hampshire history.

It's dated about 1930.'' Irene reached into her desk drawer and retrieved a thin book, opening it to a yellowed page about midway through. ''I found a mention of the Hendersons, all right, but they're just a footnote.''

With a soft chuckle, Emily accepted the thesis from her. ''I guess that's better than being totally ignored.'' Like the local historians had managed to do.

At the bottom of the open page she discovered a note indicating that the family of Robert Henderson, owners of three cows and two horses, had been listed in a pre-Revolutionary War census of the Honorville area. Their whereabouts and descendants were unknown as they had abandoned their property sometime prior to the next census and no records had survived.

''Well, it's nice to know the family stories that have been passed down through the years are true,'' Emily said, though the word *abandoned* struck her as implying the departure had been unplanned. ''At least as far as this goes. As I recall, the family moved to Vermont and eventually settled in upper New York raising apples.''

''Why don't you browse through the book?'' Ms. Carver suggested. ''I'm sorry I can't check it out to you. University rules.''

''No problem. I'll read it here.''

She found a seat near the gentleman reading the *New York Times*. It looked like he hadn't moved since the last time she'd visited the library. He still wore the same gray, rumpled suit. She imagined the man was a permanent fixture, one who didn't return her friendly smile.

The thesis was fascinating, containing more details about who did what to whom in the early history of New Hampshire than she had ever imagined uncovering. One passage she found particularly intriguing. A group of New Hampshire irregulars had been ambushed en route to join General Washington's Continental Army. There was an indication that local Tory informers, working under the direction of a British major named Hussey, had been responsible for the attack, but no charges had ever been brought.

That suggested to Emily that a spy ring of sorts had operated in the area—but not under a Captain Witherspoon. Major Hussey was the man in charge.

The news only deepened her unsettled feelings about Cal. Could he possibly have read this account and, with some strange shifting of logic, adopted the experience as his own? That hardly seemed reasonable. At the moment, she couldn't decide if she was glad or not there was no reference to a Captain Witherspoon. Whatever was the truth, Cal had certainly gotten under her skin—if not into her bed.

When she finished reading the thesis, she realized she'd already missed the chance to pick up Pete before he got on the bus for home. She'd have to hurry to be there when he arrived.

Outside she discovered the rain had turned to snow, heavy and thick, blowing up a real nor'easter. She zipped up her jacket. The weatherman hadn't predicted snow, much less a blizzard. But then, what did they know?

Roads slicked with several inches of snow greeted her as she exited the library parking lot. Mounds, like white meringue, topped fence posts and weighed down branches still dotted with colorful leaves. Driving was treacherous. Her windshield wipers flailed away at the blowing snow with little effect. Even moving at a snail's pace, the car slid at every corner, or whenever she put on the brakes.

Welcome to a New England winter, she thought grimly. The snow tires she'd bought were barely keeping her on the road.

She made her way cautiously through town and headed up the road to Henderson House, making it a point to keep her wheels in tracks already traveled by prior vehicles. Lord knew when the Highway Department plows would show up. Soon, she hoped. Based on her research, snow shouldn't have fallen in serious amounts for another month.

So much for research, she concluded.

As she approached the hill near her house, she accelerated. Though she didn't have much experience driving on snow, she knew if she slowed too much she'd never be able to reach the top.

Visibility was dismal. She'd just trust to luck that no other car was foolish enough to be out on the road in this mess. Perhaps she should have arranged to stay somewhere in town until the roads were cleared.

Too late she spotted the square yellow back of the school bus. It loomed in front of her, half on the road and half off.

She applied the brakes, and the car slithered to a stop just as the bumper tapped the back of the bus. She let out a sigh. She was now in no better shape than the bus, which looked to be thoroughly stuck. The only good news was that she wasn't far from home.

Getting out of the car, she trudged through the snow and knocked on the door of the bus.

A panicky-looking adolescent appeared on the other side of the glass. A moment later the door opened.

"Can you help us?" the boy asked. "We're stuck rock solid and the driver...I think he broke his arm or somethin' when we slid off the road. Some of the kids wanted to walk home, but I told 'em we got to stay—"

"You did absolutely the right thing." As she climbed into the bus, fear clutched at Emily's stomach. A busload of kids in a blizzard? She wasn't any more prepared for that kind of an emergency than was the teenage kid.

"Hey, Mom, is that you?" Pete appeared out of the murky dusk from the back of the bus.

Relieved, she gave him a hug. Her son was safe. "It's okay, honey. We're almost home."

She turned to the driver. The poor man's face was ashen from the pain and he held his right arm in his lap. There was a bloody gash on his forehead. He didn't look like he would be much help, under the circumstances.

Placing her hand on his shoulder, she said, "Do you think either the boy or I could drive this bus back onto the road?"

His eyes unfocused, he looked up at her. "Not a chance. The right wheels ... they're off the shoulder. It'll take—" He bit his lip against the pain. "We'll need a tow truck. One o' them big 'uns."

Swell. What was she supposed to do now?

She looked around. Six kids were still on the bus, and the oldest was the fifteen-year-old who'd met her at the door. The rest were younger. A few more inches of snow and they'd never be able to navigate through the blowing drifts.

She clicked off the options in her mind. The bus was warm enough for the moment, but that wouldn't last long. It might be hours before a plow arrived. Darkness was falling fast. If she was going to act, it had to be now. Henderson House was no more than five hundred yards away—she hoped.

"What's your name?" she asked the teenager.

"Steven. Steve Carver."

"Irene Carver's son? The librarian?"

"Yes, ma'am."

She could see in his dark eyes he understood their dilemma. "Okay, Steve. My house is just up at the top of the hill, off to the right. Do you think you're strong enough to get the bus driver that far?"

He swallowed hard. "Yes, ma'am. I think so."

She hoped to God she was making the right decision. "Okay, kids," she said to the rest of the bus, "we're all going to my house. It's not far. Then we'll call your parents to tell them you're safe."

She sorted out the youngsters, pairing them up as best she could in a buddy system. She took the hand of the smallest girl and assigned Pete to the next youngest. Steve managed to get the bus driver on his feet and out of the vehicle.

Once outside the bus, she realized how quickly the temperature had plummeted. The kids would all be frostbitten within minutes if she didn't get them safely to her house. The wind-driven arctic air snaked under her jacket and snapped at her ears, freezing her face and hands. The landscape blurred. They trudged upward, an eerie entourage, bearing right at the break in the rock wall that led to her house.

Not far now, she told herself as the child next to her stumbled. Just keep going.

Out of the gloom the figure of a man appeared. Large. Imposing. Powerful. Wearing a familiar maroon jacket emblazoned with the words *Honorville High*. A more welcome sight than she could have thought possible.

"Cal." The wind whipped the soft whisper of his name from her lips.

He hefted her leg-weary young charge into his arms. "I've been fair worried about you, luv. Seems you have brought a few guests for the inn."

"I don't think they're paying customers," she said. For a moment she leaned against his broad shoulder, not sure either she or the children would have had the strength and endurance to make the last few hundred yards without his help. He smelled of winter crispness, soap and the lingering traces of his sweet pipe tobacco. "Let's get the kids inside."

Cal urged and cajoled the children forward until they plodded their way to the house, shivering and shaking in their too-light autumn jackets, which were not meant to protect against the ravages of an early, unpredicted winter storm.

On shaky legs, Emily headed for the phone. The children's parents were no doubt frantic with worry.

The bus was already late. She wanted to reassure them all was well.

She picked up the instrument only to discover the line was dead.

"Damn," she muttered, grateful her own son was safely home. Rural New England living wasn't all peaches and cream.

With little other choice, Emily prepared soup and grilled cheese sandwiches for the children's dinner. Later, she assigned them rooms upstairs where they would spend the night. Meanwhile, Cal managed to splint the bus driver's arm, tend his head wound and put young Steven in charge of the younger students. The boy seemed quite pleased with the responsibility.

Somewhere in the midst of all the confusion, it occurred to Emily that Cal was a natural leader. He delegated responsibilities. Was calm in the face of adversity. And everyone paid attention to what he said.

"All right, luv. It is your turn now." He took her by the shoulders and turned Emily away from the kitchen sink. "All of the young lads and lassies are safely tucked in their beds and the driver is resting."

"I still have the dishes—"

"We'll organize a work crew in the morning. It will keep them all out of mischief." He dried her hands on a tea towel. "Right now, you are going upstairs to have a long soak in the tub."

"A bath?"

"Aye. I have already drawn the water for you, luv." He palmed her cheek and gazed at her with such intensity it made her breath catch. What hid behind his dark beard? she wondered. A dimple? A cleft? Would she ever know?

"You didn't have to—"

"But I did. You are bone weary from your ordeal and your insides are probably still chilled from the storm."

That wasn't quite true. Standing this close to Cal, his hand lightly caressing her cheek, was doing a number on her internal temperature gauge that would have melted an iceberg.

"You don't have to pamper me, Cal. I'm perfectly capable—"

Deep grooves settled across his forehead. "When the storm came and you were late getting back, I was worried. More than that, I admit. I have fought off bands of Continentals, and skulked around in the bushes to avoid having my head blown off. At times as a lad I managed to face down my father. I even stood strong at the gallows.... But today, lass..." He drew a deep breath and his trembling fingers gently mapped the contours of her face. "Today, for the first time, I was truly frightened."

His velvet voice admitting the depth of his concern tugged seductively at Emily's inner core. She felt trapped between the kitchen counter and his overpowering virility, her heart already hopelessly captured. Her hands slipped up to press against his chest. Awareness of the rhythm of his heart swept over her. It marked the same heavy tempo she felt in her chest, and which pulsed much lower in her body.

She'd been down this route with Cal before. The last time he'd drawn a line she hadn't been able to cross. Surely this time...

"I was afraid for the children," she admitted, surprised at the husky timbre of her voice.

"I should not have let you go off alone." His thumb outlined her lower lip, flesh rubbing against flesh.

"No one predicted the storm." She'd be the first to predict a maelstrom of pleasure if only Cal would surrender to the feelings she was sure he had for her. His body heat seemed to leap the narrow gap that separated them. Her breasts felt heavy, achy and filled with need.

In a fluid motion, Calvert lifted and cradled Emily in his arms, an action born of his need to hold her.

She gasped in surprise.

"No more arguments, luv. It is time for you to be pampered, and there is no better candidate than I for the job." The afternoon had indeed been the worst in his life. He had imagined all kinds of dire consequences of the sudden storm, and when he had set out to find her, and did so quickly, his relief had known no bounds. Now that he had her safely back, he vowed to cherish her as no other man ever could, though that, he realized, would never be enough.

"I'm not so tired I can't walk," she protested softly, her face nestled at the crook of his neck.

"Give me the privilege of indulging you this once."

"Hmm," she purred. "Permission granted."

He pushed out through the kitchen door and carried her up the stairway, walking silently past closed bedrooms where their guests slept for the night. The house was still, as quiet as it had been when Calvert had roamed through the emptiness alone. In years gone by, he had only the wind whistling through the gables for company. Now, he had Emily.

He never wanted to let her go. Ghosts were not supposed to feel such gut-wrenching hunger and need. He did. There was no point in denying it any longer. And he certainly didn't want to risk a bloke like Berrington crowding into her life.

Crooking her arm more firmly around Cal's neck, Emily delighted in the flex and ripple of his muscles beneath her hand. His power was channeled, controlled with a gentleness that hid the extent of his strength. Exploring a little further, her fingers discovered the waves of his dark, silken hair curling over his shirt collar. Weaving her fingers through the lush strands was fully as self-indulgent as consuming a box of rich chocolates and perhaps just as foolish. Or addictive.

When they entered the bedroom, she felt him shift her position slightly, holding her even more tightly against him. Then she heard the click of the key in the lock.

"So no one will disturb your soak in the tub," he explained, his voice so low and husky she felt the vibration shimmer down her spine.

She tried to suppress a heated shiver of anticipation rising within her. "Good idea." Particularly with Cal on her side of the door.

In the bathroom, he slowly lowered her to her feet, her body following the contours of his chest, narrow waist and lean hips until she stood solidly once again.

Separated only by two thicknesses of clothing, she felt the contact of their bodies in a dozen places. Each spot became a candle flame that grew and flickered more brightly by the moment.

Surely this time he wouldn't call a halt to things before they got fully started. She didn't think she could take another dose of false hope.

"Off with your clothes, lass," he ordered. His pulse beat wildly in his throat and his groin ached. Calvert knew this bath was going to take all of his control, yet he was doggedly determined to pamper his lady. Surely a two-hundred-year sentence served as a ghost gave him that right, if nothing more.

He lifted the edge of her sweater.

"You're going to undress me?" Her question quavered and echoed in the room.

"Aye. It is part of the pampering."

"How . . . nice."

As he skimmed the sweater past her midriff, she raised her arms. She felt a languorous sensation weight her limbs while the fabric moved sensuously along her flesh. He caught her hands for a moment above her head, making her feel thoroughly exposed, then tossed away the sweater. Slowly, he trailed the back of his hand down the inside of her arm, flesh she hadn't realized could be so extraordinarily sensitive.

She licked her lips. "You're very good at this," she whispered. When he put his mind to it, seduction was Cal's middle name. She'd sensed that from the beginning.

"I have had some small experience."

She would have laughed but the sound caught in her throat. He was already busy working the zipper on her jeans.

"The shoes have to come off first," she managed to say.

One eyebrow raised, he studied the problem. "I see I must alter my technique a bit to suit modern costumes."

He slid the jeans down over her hips, his work-roughened hands skimming the curving swell, then lowered her to sit on the chilled edge of the tub. Kneeling, he removed her shoes and socks one by one. There was an artistry to each movement, a seductive brush of hand against calf, a caress of the arch, a stroke of the sensitive skin around the ankle.

"You learn very quickly, Cal." She was trembling when he finished.

"A natural talent, I assure you."

She imagined so. And it didn't bother her in the least. Even the hoarseness of his voice was another caress against her already overheated flesh.

Cupping her elbow, he raised her to her feet again. For a moment, he inspected her lacy bra and bikini panties, all that she now wore. She felt no embarrassment. Only the swirling of hot, burning need throughout her body.

"Undergarments are much less confining these days, to my great delight. Some of those bones and corsets proved a decided challenge with other matters on a man's mind." Canting his lips into a grin, he gave her a thoroughly masculine appraisal that sizzled clear down to her toes. "This arrangement is much more to my taste."

"I'm glad you approve."

"But women have changed little over the years."

"Basic genetics." And a good deal of lust, which was probably ageless. She could feel the desire curling through her abdomen, the same sensation women of all generations had experienced for the man they loved.

The mechanics of her bra posed little problem for Cal. It landed on the heap of her clothes, as did her bikini undies.

Feeling more weak-kneed by the moment, she held on to his shoulders to steady herself. "Cal, just how far are we going with this?"

"Patience, my dear." He placed a silencing finger on her lips. "First, your bath." Reaching across her, he turned the hot water on full force. "I fear the water has cooled."

Lord, she was so hot she could probably steam an entire lake dry. Sweat sheened on her forehead and glowed in the valley between her breasts.

She glanced at the tub and swallowed hard. "Bubbles?"

"Rather a nice touch, don't you think? I found a container on the counter."

One she'd bought on a whim years ago, an extravagant product she'd packed with her personal items in California. She'd never before taken the time to indulge herself. Perhaps, in the back of her mind, she'd hoped...

The subtle scent of roses drifted up to mix with the steam.

He urged her into the tub, and the bubbles settled around her like a warm, sensuous blanket. She felt a tremor of sheer, decadent pleasure.

Chapter Eleven

"You're spoiling me."

"I have not even yet begun." Calvert dipped a cloth into the water and drizzled the suds across Emily's shoulders. With a stifled groan, he watched in envy as the bubbles trailed along her fair skin. He wanted to be that close, to follow the same path leading beneath the water to where the dusky rose of her nipples beckoned in shadow.

"Amazing what I've missed by taking quick showers."

"There are some things that should not be rushed." Like learning the shape of Emily's body, each feminine curve and lush swell. His slow study with cloth and hand was sweet torture, intensifying an ache that had only one cure. "A nice soak is always relaxing after a hard day."

She licked her lips. Her throat felt dry. And hot, like the rest of her body. "Relaxation isn't exactly what I'm experiencing."

"Hmm." He lifted her leg, smoothing the cloth over her arch, her calf, and farther up the sensitive flesh of her thigh. "Perhaps I have forgotten some of the finer points."

"I doubt that." The cloth swept over her stomach to the hidden triangle of hair and then down to the soft flesh below. Her muscles clenched. A soft sound escaped her throat.

"Relaxing may have been a poor choice of words," he conceded.

Substitute seducing, exciting or tantalizing, she thought. Or all of the above.

He withdrew the cloth in a slow, intimate caress that made her dizzy with desire. She gripped his wrist but not to ward him off. Rather, she simply needed to touch him.

"Easy, luv. There's another leg to be done."

"Cal..." she whispered faintly.

Methodically, he began the seduction of her left leg. Somehow the cloth was no longer there. Only his hand, the width of his palm, skimming her flesh in long, heated strokes. Waves lapped against her aching breasts in an exquisite imitation of his caress.

Calvert sought again the sweet, secret warmth of Emily's womanhood. Never in his life had he been so tested. It was not as though the sight of a naked woman was new to him. Indeed the shape and form were quite familiar. Or so he had thought until now.

With Emily he discovered a unique combination of delicacy and strength, both in mind and body. He found the blending of the two as intoxicating as fine brandy. He inhaled deeply, as he would savor the bouquet before tasting the flavor of wine. Roses. In some other life, he would remember the scent and think of her.

The bathing continued, his hands mapping her firm breasts and the sweet, sensitive flesh beneath her arms. Pleasure such as he had never before known ripped through him.

Standing, he lifted a towel from the rack. "Out you come, luv."

Taking his hand, she stood a little shakily. Her body glistened with moisture, a perfection of soft, rounded curves and deep valleys inviting his further exploration.

"Lovely," he murmured, wrapping the towel under her arms and across her breasts, hiding those secret places he most wanted to admire.

"You got your shirt wet." With trembling fingers, she worked the top button loose.

He covered her hand, halting her attempts to undress him. "My task with you is not yet complete."

"No?" She certainly felt about as ready as a woman could. Patience was not her long suit. Not when her body tingled with desire.

"Nay, for you are a woman who has been seriously deprived of late, and I intend to make up for that to the best of my ability."

"All in one night?"

His lips quirked. "Would you doubt my skills?" he asked dryly.

Not a chance. She just wasn't sure how much more of his seduction she could stand with her heart threatening to burst in her chest and the coiling heat radiating through her body. She was melting from the inside out.

"Do you perchance have some bath oil?" he asked.

"Under the sink. I thought if winter got too dry..." She watched him retrieve the bottle from the cupboard. "Cal, I don't think—"

"My sweet, stubborn, practical Emily," he sighed. "In these matters, it is wisest not to think at all. I assure you this entire process is as natural as breathing."

That might well be true for him, but Emily was having trouble drawing a single breath. Surely a woman wouldn't forget something as basic as that. She never had before, she thought dimly, trying to reassure herself.

He led her to the bedroom, pulled down the covers and ordered her to lie down on her stomach. The sheet felt cold on her overheated flesh. She lay there a moment, every nerve ending alive with the heady thrill of anticipation.

Calvert poured a little of the oil into his palms and sat down beside Emily. When he began to rub up and down on her body, relishing the friction of flesh upon flesh, she muttered a contented sound into the pillow.

Slowly, expertly, he expanded the area that now glowed with the sweet-smelling oil. His hands slicked to the side, just brushing against the fullness of her breasts, then slid to her waist and back again. Each exploration took him a little lower, to the satin curve of her hip, teasing near the velvet cleft.

She made another throaty sound.

"Too much?" he asked with a smile.

"Yes... No." She sighed.

The sight of his hands moving freely across her buttocks was sweet torment, knotting his loins into a stiffness that pushed painfully against the fabric of his trousers.

"Cal?" Her breath broke on a ragged sigh.

For a moment, he didn't answer. He couldn't until the gripping need relaxed its claim on him.

"Aye, luv. What is it you wish?"

"Calvert, has anyone ever told you it's possible to go too slow?"

"Not that I can recall."

She turned onto her back. "Kiss me, Cal. Make love to me."

"That's what I have been doing, lass, since first I set eyes on you. I had not thought it possible how much I would come to want you."

The bed lamp cast an angled shadow across his rugged features as his head lowered to hers. She lifted her arms in welcome.

At first he teased her with chaste kisses, peppering her lips with only the flick of his tongue, first at one corner and then the other. She tried to pull him closer but he resisted her efforts, continuing his frustrating onslaught that only made her more anxious to fully taste his lips.

"Cal?"

"Aye, lass. Is there something more you would like?" Beneath his hooded lids there lay a twinkle of mischief.

"You devil." He silenced her throaty laugh with a deep kiss that took her breath away. She savored the taste of his passionate surrender.

As though there was still oil on his hands, he visited all those parts of her as yet untouched. Her nipples hardened, her breasts ached. The flower of need burst to full bloom when his hand flattened across his stomach and his fingers dipped for the tender folds just below.

"Cal, you're not...playing...fair," she complained between sharp little gasps of pleasure.

"How's that?"

"Your clothes. You're wearing too many."

"Ah, yes. A detail I apparently overlooked."

"I'd appreciate it if you would rectify the situation." She drew in another shuddering breath. "Soon."

He needed little assistance in solving the problem and no more encouragement. Thank goodness. All Emily had to do was admire his physique as each new portion was revealed in the small circle of light from the bed lamp. He was all she had imagined. And more. Smooth of muscle. Tight, masculine butt, with the faintest white scar on the right side. Dark hair covering his chest and arrowing to the nest that showed him to be a magnificent male specimen.

Lord, she'd be able to look at Cal every day for the rest of her life and still find something new to admire.

When he returned to Emily, Cal set his mouth, lips and tongue to work traveling the same territory once visited so expertly by his hands. But now she could enjoy the tactile feel of his flesh brushing against hers, the sensuous movement of his beard, like the finest sandpaper sensitizing her skin.

She kneaded his shoulders and back, dampened with a fine sheen of sweat. She tasted the musky bass note of his skin. Through it all, her body responded to his fiery magic until she could stand it no longer.

"Cal. Now. Please." Instinctively, she arched her back, seeking the ultimate fulfillment she knew he would provide.

He paused above her for a dozen thundering beats of his heart. This was the final test. Was it possible that for two hundred years he had been wrong about his abilities...his needs? Or had things changed only with Emily's arrival? If he failed her now...

He gritted his teeth. He would not even consider that possibility.

With a strangled cry of determination, he sheathed himself in her warm, moist cavern. She arched beneath him and called out his name.

"So good, luv."

"Yes, oh, yes."

She moved with him, eagerly catching his rhythm, adding her own, letting him fill her more deeply. He raised her hips and she locked her legs around his waist. By all that was holy, never had it been this good, not through all eternity.

Kissing her face, her throat, he listened to her eager cries of pleasure and heard his own echoing response. He kneaded her breasts, her hips, all of her silken flesh as her fingernails raked at his back.

He felt her spasm tightly around him, again and again, her cries of release muffled in his mouth. What little remained of his control snapped, sending him over the edge. He tumbled into a deep, welcoming abyss, his heart pounding so hard he feared it might shake the whole house.

Emily held him, cherishing his weight, the length of him touching along her legs, across her pelvis, pressing against her breasts, his warm breath caressing her neck where his head rested at her shoulder. Calvert T. Witherspoon. An enigma in so much that he said and did. The man she loved. She had no idea what tomorrow might bring. But for tonight she was content.

He heard her sigh and rolled to his back, pulling her into his arms again. His chest pillowed her head as she smoothed the curly, dark hair that grew there, each strand a midnight black. She loved the feel of him, his textured flesh, the exquisite combination of muscle and sinew that rippled beneath her fingertips.

"How old are you, Cal?"

"Hmm. About two hundred and forty—"

"That's not what I mean." She tweaked one of the hairs on his chest.

"Ouch." He grabbed her hand. "I gather that answer didn't suit you. Perhaps I can do better. The last birthday I celebrated was my thirty-second."

"Oh," she responded self-consciously. "I'm thirty-five. Does that bother you?"

"That you are much older than I?" There was a smile in his voice. "It matters little since you are so well preserved."

Laughing, she said, "Thanks a lot." She'd asked for that one. "Cal?"

"Another question?"

"Women like to talk after having good sex."

"Is that so? Then I shall view this conversation as a compliment."

"Hmm." He didn't need any more praise for his lovemaking. His skill and technique, along with her reactions, spoke for themselves. Eloquently. "When you were spying for England...did you arrange an ambush of some New Hampshire irregulars?"

His silence lasted so long she thought perhaps he'd drifted off to sleep.

"I fear my efforts in the war were not very successful. Then again, perhaps it is just as well I was not responsible for the loss of any of your countrymen." He ran his hand along her upper arm. "It is possible my superior, Major Hussey, arranged such a venture after I was hung. There had been some discussion of the subject."

Emily became very still. "You knew Major Hussey?" The same one she'd read about at the library?

"Aye. Better than I would have liked. He was the bloke who was so anxious to see me dancing on the gallows."

No, it wasn't true. Dammit! The man had just shown her with exquisite clarity that he couldn't possibly be a ghost. Yet he seemed to know obscure historical details that only a careful researcher—or someone who'd been there—would know.

Closing her eyes, she snuggled more closely against his warm, human heat. She simply didn't have the energy right now to deal with a problem that seemed to have no rational equation, particularly since Cal's fingertip had begun making delicious circles along the side of her breast.

He brushed a kiss to her damp forehead. "It seems my recuperative powers have been little damaged by long abstinence."

She slid her hand down his flat stomach to discover the truth of his words. "Again?"

"I fear in my eagerness to possess you, I may have rushed a bit too much. To redress the error—" he rolled her onto her back "—I shall endeavor to proceed even more slowly this time."

"More slowly?" He muffled her echoed words with a deep, lingering kiss. Clearly, Cal had in mind to *pamper* her to death. What a wonderful way to go....

MORNING IN THE KITCHEN resembled Camp Runamuck for kids.

"What do you mean, you don't like cereal?" Emily asked. In frustration, she blew a drooping strand of hair back from her forehead. Sleep had been in short supply last night. Not that she'd minded—far from it—but it did mean her patience with fussy eaters was extra-thin. If it hadn't been for the satisfied little smile that kept creeping up her cheeks, she might really have been quite short with the children.

"My mommy fixes me eggs every morning. Scrambled. I don't like them runny." Stephanie lifted her chin and puffed out her lower lip. "Bacon, too."

"Sweetie, in this house I've got cereal and toast. You can have either or both, but there aren't enough eggs for everyone." She gave the child a pat on the head. "Your choice." Hadn't her mother ever heard about cholesterol?

"Good morning, lads and lassies." Cal strolled into the room calm as you please, wearing his familiar jeans and flannel shirt. His hair was slightly damp, as though he'd just come from the shower. "Did you all have a good rest?"

The youngsters chorused an affirmative response.

"Then 'tis time to get ourselves organized." He gave Emily a slow wink that made her heart skip up to her throat. "Pete, lad, you know your way around the kitchen, so you find the bowls for your friends and the boxes of cereal. Steven, you are in charge of pouring the milk. And Becky, my favorite little lass, you tell your mother when the toast is ready."

The children scurried to do his bidding.

Cal turned to Emily. "Do we have enough juice to go round?"

"I think so." She noted his use of the proprietary "we" and smiled.

"It might be just as well if you did the honors with the juice. Spills, you know."

"I quite agree, Captain."

Stephanie tugged on his sleeve. "I don't like cereal."

"Is that a fact?" He took her hand and led her to a seat at the table. "I recall the time my lads and I were out on patrol. We got a bit lost, I fear, and found ourselves without victuals for three days. When we finally arrived back at camp, the mess had stirred up buckets of turnips—"

"Yucky. I don't like—"

"Neither do I, lass." He pulled out the chair for her. "But you know, never had anything tasted so good.

Indeed, my stomach was quite relieved to discover my throat hadn't been slit and was therefore more than happy to receive something as detestable as turnips."

The child giggled and within moments had filled her bowl with cereal.

"You're a wonder, Cal," Emily whispered once the children were more or less settled and eating.

"'Tis an easy thing to think like a child when you are not quite grown-up yourself."

"You're all the man I'll ever be able to handle."

He caught her meaning, and a satisfied smile quirked his lips. "That, luv, is another matter altogether." His voice spread warmly over her like tropical mist.

She slid her arm around his waist. He was so sturdy, so thoroughly honorable and caring, her heart filled with love. Never before had she felt the need to lean on a man. Her marriage had been a partnership of two equals. Entirely satisfactory at the time.

But somehow here in New Hampshire she had changed. The realization made her feel extraordinarily vulnerable.

How could she possibly rely on Cal when he continued to be convinced he was a ghost? And his stories rang loudly with the truth of that conviction.

Yet at the same time, she had never experienced such total pleasure and satisfaction in a man's arms. The memory of the night past rippled through Emily, bringing with it a tingling sensation. Cal was so thoroughly human it simply wasn't possible to think of him in any other way.

The jangling phone startled her. The lines had evidently been repaired.

When she answered, the caller identified himself as Herb Marlow, Superintendent of Honorville School District.

"Mrs. Morrell, we've had a report the school bus is off the road near your house. We're hoping—"

"The children are all safe, Mr. Marlow. They're eating breakfast right now."

She could hear his relief as he thanked her and hung up.

A half hour later, a procession of cars, led by the snowplow, rumbled up her driveway. Snow was still falling, though the wind had eased considerably and the temperature had risen to near freezing.

Mothers and fathers crowded into the entryway as the children sorted out their jackets and schoolbooks. An elderly woman helped the bus driver to her car, promising to take him right to the doctor.

Irene Carver gave Emily a hug. "We're all so relieved."

"I know," she replied. "Your son, by the way, was an absolute rock. Without his help, the bus driver never would have been able to make it to the house."

The librarian beamed with pride and her eyes glistened with unshed tears. "He's a good boy."

"Mrs. Morrell, we can't thank you enough," another mother began.

"Please call me Emily. And I'm only sorry the phones were out. I know how worried you all must have been."

"I hope Stephanie wasn't a problem for you." The stocky woman looked very much like her daughter. "She's at a stage—"

"She was fine. The kids even helped clean up the kitchen." Under Cal's careful supervision.

"Mercy, my Robbie won't do a speck of work at home," one mother said and laughed, hugging her son for about the tenth time in as many minutes.

"It was Cal's doing. He had them all quite well organized." Emily reached out and took his hand, bringing Cal into the middle of the group. "I'm not sure you have all met Calvert Witherspoon. He's..." How should she introduce him? As the Henderson ghost? Her lover? Neither choice seemed appropriate at the moment. "He's been helping me with the restoration of Henderson House."

There were handshakes all around, more thank yous, and then final goodbyes. Emily and Cal followed the families as far as the porch.

When the last car edged out of sight, Emily leaned back against a pillar.

"Whew. I think I remember now why I only had two children. What a zoo!"

"They were a good lot." Smiling, he brushed a straying bit of hair away from her face. "As for me, I always thought a large family would be best. Six or eight children seemed a nice number."

She rolled her eyes heavenward. "No thanks. I'll stick with two, if you don't mind."

He lifted her chin, turning her head from side to side, frowning as he inspected her.

"What's wrong?" she asked.

"Something happened to your face, luv? 'Tis all red."

Touching her cheek, she said, "I think that's called whisker burn. Fortunately, none of the children noticed. Or, at least, they didn't say anything."

"My beard did that to you?"

"I don't mind." It had been worth every delicious moment.

"I should have realized how sensitive your skin is. You are so very fair and lovely." He placed a gentle kiss on her jaw. "The whiskers will be gone by bedtime."

"You don't have to shave for me." She palmed his cheek and rubbed her hand along his beard.

"Yes, I do. Never would I knowingly hurt you, lass."

"If that's what you want." Reaching up, she kissed him firmly on the mouth. He tasted of sweet morning coffee. "Just remember, tonight it's your turn."

He raised a questioning eyebrow.

"Tonight I'm going to pamper *you*."

"I TELL YOU she knows something."

"That's not possible."

"It was that Carver woman. She tracked down a reference to the Hendersons in some other fool library."

"How do you know that?"

"Dammit, woman! I was there!"

"No need to shout. Besides, whatever she found won't mean anything to her."

"It will if she found out about the ambush, too."

The woman leaned heavily against the counter. "Do you have any idea what that would do to our business if word got out?"

The second man swore under his breath. "Your other stupid plan sure didn't work worth beans."

"Whose fault is that?"

"I did the best I could. Can I help it if Emily—"

"Maybe we ought to forget the whole idea."

"You can say that easy 'nough. It wouldn't be dollars oot of your pocket."

"Come on. If we start fighting among ourselves we'll never solve the problem. We've got the whole economic future of Honorville resting on our shoulders."

"Not to mention my next political campaign."

Chapter Twelve

Calvert folded his arms across his chest and leaned against the doorjamb of one of the upstairs guest rooms. A smile tugged at his lips as he watched Emily at work. Even performing a mundane task like hanging wallpaper, she was beautiful. And determined.

"Are you going to be at that all day?" he asked, observing the way her jeans gloved the familiar curve of her hips.

"I'd like to finish the rest of the room by tonight." With a dry brush, she carefully smoothed the damp edge of the floral-print paper. "Are the kids gone?"

"Pete left on the bus, as scheduled, and Becky is off with her new chum from art class."

"Thanks."

Turning Henderson House into what Emily called a bed and breakfast was an obsession with her, Calvert mused. The only time she relented was when she was in his arms, a position they had enjoyed each of the last seven nights since they had first made love. A gratifying position, he mentally amended. One he intended to repeat very soon with a variation on the same general theme.

Odd how he had come to need her so much in such a short time. Troubling, too.

The thought of ever having to leave her gnawed at the back of his mind like an insistent rash. Worse, the possibility that she would grow old and die in the natural course of things, leaving him to haunt the earth alone, twisted through his gut like a saber driven to its hilt.

Bloody hell! What a jumble he had made of things, and now there was no turning back. He needed her too much to simply walk away.

In two short strides, he was behind her, pulling her hard against him, his forearm settling under her full breasts. She was soft and pliable and his for as long as he could hold her.

She gasped. "Cal, don't—"

He silenced her with a nipping kiss on the column of her neck, followed by an exploration with his tongue around the delicate folds of her ear.

"I'm all..." Trembling, she leaned back, tilting her head to bare her throat more readily to his kisses. "I smell of glue."

"An interesting fragrance, my dear. In its own way quite enticing on you."

"Don't be ridiculous. There's nothing sexy about a woman putting up wallpaper."

"Let me be the judge of that, luv."

She turned in his arms to gaze lovingly into blue eyes darkened with ill-concealed passion—a reflection of her own, Emily suspected. Though she might always miss his beard, the crease in his clean-shaven cheek when he smiled brought a lump to her throat. God, he was good-looking. She loved his rugged, outdoorsy look, but she imagined in a coat and tie he could as easily model for *GQ*.

He was talented, too. She remembered the way, each time they had made love, his hands caressed her with such skill, the seductive taste of his lips, the agonizing way he forced her tension to build until she cried out his name in utter abandon. She'd never before felt so totally uninhibited with a man. Nor had she been so pleased to find that she could give as much pleasure as she received.

After all these years, she discovered she liked the role of aggressor from time to time. Variety certainly added a good many sparks to the bedroom scene.

Hot stuff, she thought with a smirking smile.

"Ah, you are thinking about how it is with us," Cal said, his grin widening.

Heat slid up her neck. "How did you know?"

"'Tis in your eyes, lass. They always tell me what excites you."

"Clever of you to notice." She'd never been very good at keeping secrets. In this case, she didn't want to.

"Hmm." He ran a single finger along the line between her ear and chin. "For instance, when I do that, I know it pleases you."

"Yes," she sighed. Everything about Cal pleased her.

"And when my hand does thusly..." He slid his palm across the top of her breast, then cupped it from below, lifting its weight. "...your pupils grow large with the desire you feel."

"So do yours." Like black agates.

"Your body responds to mine." He demonstrated by flicking his thumb across her nipple. It reacted instantly to his touch. "In places where I cannot see, your excitement builds. A tightening in your stomach?"

"You know that's what happens." Rapid heartbeat and accelerated breathing were a couple of other frequent symptoms when she was around Cal. Like at this very moment.

He pulled her hard against his chest, letting his arousal press against her abdomen. "And when you feel me wanting you in this way, your eyes tell me you are ready for a new adventure."

"Adventure?" She swallowed hard, imagining being ravished while wrapped up cocoonlike in wallpaper. Not a good plan. "Maybe we ought to wait."

He removed the brush from her hand and carefully placed it across the can of glue. "'Tis a glorious day outside, full of sunlight."

"It's still near freezing." Though he'd done a pretty darn good job of raising her internal temperature by several degrees.

"With what I have in mind, you won't be cold."

She could feel some of that heat right now. "But, Cal—"

"Hush, luv. There's a place I want to show you. With the children gone, now is our chance. I have packed us some bread and cheese and a bottle of wine. We'll have ourselves a bit of a picnic."

"We just had breakfast."

His eyes glistened with devilment. "I believe I can offer some rather satisfying entertainment that will last until we are hungry again."

Wrapping her arms around his waist and resting her head against his broad chest, she said, "I hope you realize you are a bad influence, Captain Witherspoon. We have so much to do—"

"There will be the whole winter to do it in." He placed a kiss on her forehead so lightly it felt like little more than a soft summer breeze. "As Peter once suggested, my dear, playing hooky offers its own reward."

Cal was right, Emily decided as they walked hand in hand along a path leading away from the burned-out carriage house. He carried a wicker basket he'd found in the attic, and a blanket was tossed casually over his shoulder. With a flight of fancy that took little imagination, she knew exactly who would end up on that blanket and what they would be doing. The thought accelerated her heartbeat.

Would she never get enough of the man? Cal was as addictive as the most powerful drug and had the same affect as megavitamins. She had never felt so full of good health and energy. A daily, or nightly, dose of Calvert T. Witherspoon seemed just about right, though she found she wasn't averse to accepting an extra helping.

The air had an invigorating bite that tingled her cheeks. For the most part, the early snow had already melted, leaving only a few patches of glistening white in shaded spots. The trees had lost their leaves. From the red and gold of autumn, the landscape had changed into starkly contrasting shades of dark and light. Bare maple branches stretched in winter silence toward a blue sky hazed with wispy clouds. All around her was the scent of rich, moist soil and the stillness of anticipation.

"Did you often play hooky from school?" she asked, noting the contrast between the size and texture of their hands, his tapered fingers laced alternately with hers.

"I was taught by tutors, I fear. Devilishly hard to escape them. Though I confess I was successful a time or two."

Walking in step together, Cal's long strides shortened to match hers, their feet created a soft, rhythmic sound on top of the fallen leaves. Their jeans brushing together, thigh to thigh, made an intimate swishing noise. "You didn't enjoy your studies?"

"I enjoyed less getting whacked on my knuckles, I assure you. The young men my father employed were dreadfully boring aesthetes who could not have found their way out of a shepherd's hut without considerable assistance."

"They couldn't have been as bad as all that."

He shrugged. "Perhaps my memory has dimmed after all this time. There were one or two who showed some spunk."

"And those you probably drove away with your mischief."

"Ah, luv, you know me too well." Laughing aloud, he squeezed her hand. His gesture had the same effect on her heart, tightening it with a band of love and contentment.

"Tell me, Mistress Morrell, was there never a time when you had to suffer the wrath of your teachers?"

"Not often," she confessed. "I once got thrown out of a high school English class for talking back to the teacher."

He assumed a shocked expression. "Surely that is not possible."

"Well, I didn't exactly mean to talk back to her. She misunderstood me."

"Now, now. No excuses, my dear," he teased. "The admission of guilt will bring us closer together. Both rotters—"

She laughed. "No. It's true. I was asking for help and she thought—"

"She rapped your knuckles for that?"

"Of course not. We don't do that anymore. I had to go see the vice principal."

His expression darkened with concern. "Did he cane you, lass?" he asked gruffly.

"Oh, Cal, you're so far behind the times." The way he worried about her warmed Emily from the inside out, as well as puzzled her. He really didn't seem to know corporal punishment had long since been banned in schools. "All I had to do was apologize to the teacher. Then everything was fine."

"But it was she who had erred."

"True. But unless I wanted to flunk the class, I had to swallow my pride."

"A more cruel punishment in its way than the cane," he observed.

The path rose up an incline, veering off to the left. Cal led her to the right on a fainter trail, past low-lying bushes and an outcropping of lichen-covered granite. So remote and unblemished was the area, Emily had the feeling they'd traveled a thousand miles from civilization, yet she knew they were less than a mile from Henderson House. No careless litter offended the eye; no graffiti marred the pristine wildness of the place. Not even the distant sound of cars on the highway could be heard.

"I hope you know where you're going," she whispered, afraid to speak aloud for fear of disrupting the eerie silence.

"Though I have not been here in many long years, I know this way as well as I know the back of my own hand."

The raspy emotion in his voice sent a shiver of anticipation down her spine. Wherever they were going, the place held memories for Cal—memories that still carried the heavy weight of pain.

A moment later they stepped out of the maple forest into a sheltered clearing surrounded by a stand of lush green spruce trees and cut by a granite creek. Along the shady edge of the slow-moving water, ice clung precariously to its promise of winter. The lightest of breezes shifted the upper spruce branches in a soft, sibilant whisper.

"Oh, my." Emily expelled the words in a sigh. She had the oddest feeling that she, too, had once visited this hidden spot. Everything looked familiar: the strangely shaped rock on the opposite bank that looked like a heart broken in half; the winter-brown flowers;

the jagged twist of an old tree stump. Only her recollection of when or how she had been here seemed fuzzed by the out-of-focus lens of her memory.

"'Tis a lovely spot, is it not?" His arm circled her waist.

A lovers' trysting place, she realized with a sharp intake of air. "You came here with Alice." It wasn't a question.

"Aye. If that bothers you—"

"No. I know she wouldn't mind." In fact, it seemed incredibly right for Emily to be here with Cal, as though it were *they* who had always arranged their secret rendezvous at this special place—not Alice and some lover from another century.

Emily shook her head. Her mind was playing fanciful tricks on her. She'd had that odd, unsettled feeling several times since she'd arrived in New Hampshire. As if Alice were actually trying to communicate with her, had gotten inside her head, just as Cal had sneaked inside her computer. Or so it had appeared.

Fortunately, she didn't believe in that sort of thing.

Still, without hesitation, she took the blanket from Cal, walked across the glade and spread the covering out on a mattress of spruce needles next to the old, jagged stump. Her stomach muscles clenched with the tight thrill of anticipation; her breathing turned shallow. It was as though the last time she had made love with Cal had been aeons ago in this same clearing, not just last night in her own four-poster bed.

Turning, she said, "Do you want to picnic first, or—"

He strolled toward her in an easy, rolling gait that accented the length of his legs and the leanness of his hips. The denim of his jeans pulled tautly across his thighs, framed by his open Windbreaker.

Emily swallowed hard.

"I find I have no appetite for bread and cheese just now," he said.

Nor did she.

He shrugged off his maroon jacket, carelessly tossing it aside. His eyes had turned a midnight black, radiating heat like coals of passion that seared across her flesh as though she were already naked.

"Cal, I'm not Alice. I don't want—"

"I have long since stopped comparing the two of you, luv. You are Emily. *My* Emily." His shirt dropped to the ground.

"Yes." Her admission slipped up her throat on a bubble of joy. She belonged to Cal. Belonged *with* Cal. Through all eternity.

Though she had seen Cal in the dim light of her bed lamp and learned the shape of his body with her hands in the darkness, she felt like she was truly seeing him for the first time. Muted shadows of spruce branches dappled his chest. Biceps that had seemed merely strong took on a steely quality that caused a ripple of what closely resembled fear to shudder through her. His flat belly was rope-hard, an impenetrable object she only wanted to caress. His chin was more square, the dark slash of his eyebrows more determined, than in the softer light of her bedroom.

He took her breath away. She'd never expected to want any man as intensely as she wanted Cal at this very moment.

In an instinctive gesture, she palmed his bare chest, delighting in the feel of her fingers plowing through the crisp hair that furred the broad expanse. His heat radiated up her arms. His heart pounded against her hand.

"Cal, this time, let's not go slow. I don't think I can stand it." She dropped her head to kiss a taut nipple on his chest, circling the rough nub with her tongue, pleased by his swift intake of air. Her hand slipped lower to the fabric that constrained Cal's swollen manhood, the part of him she wanted to feel deeply embedded within her.

"Lord, woman..." Calvert choked out the words. With an urgency he'd never before experienced, he worked at the buttons on her blouse. He wasn't sure if his greatest need was to feel her full breasts filling his hands, or to find relief from the painful pressure of clothing against his arousal.

To his great surprise, Emily mastered the snaps and buttons on his trousers before he could finish his task. He groaned at the exquisite tenderness of her fingers stroking against his sensitive member.

"If you keep that up, luv..." He'd never lost control with a woman in his life. But what Emily was doing to him, did to him almost every night, was bringing him to the brink.

As he yanked off her jacket and blouse, then released her breasts from their flimsy enclosure, he felt sweat sheening on his own forehead and chest. Lowering her trousers in a swift, sure movement, he caught the scent of her—a heady perfume that would haunt him in this life and beyond.

As he finished undressing her and laid her down on the soft wool picnic blanket, Emily was acutely aware of vibrant colors flashing through her mind—scarlets and shimmering golds—in contrast to the muted scenery around her. Their rapid breathing roared in her ears, drowning out the rippling sound of the moving water nearby. In spite of the cool air, her body seemed to be on fire, responding in a thousand heated ways to his touch—on her breasts, her stomach, at that sensitive place between her thighs.

She was drowning in sensations, each new, yet as old as time. Heat coursed through her body like a river gone wild. She stayed with the currents, riding the waves of pleasure, twisting and turning in her search for the ultimate release. Catching her breath, she sobbed at the sheer excitement that whipped her along.

There was nothing slow about their joining. It was eager, hot, all-consuming, with the power to move mountains and change the landscape of her heart and soul.

She arched up to him, accepting every hard, penetrating inch of him and asking for more. He filled her, stretched her to the limit, and then seemed to grow even larger within her.

The sound of his name bursting from Emily's throat sent a surge of pleasure through Cal that had him teetering on the edge. He sucked at one nipple and then the other, each time bringing another hungry sob to her lips. He fought for control, waited for Emily to peak, and when she spasmed around him once, twice, and then a third time, there was no hope. With a cry of un-adulterated joy, he spilled his seed deeply within her.

The silence of the glade settled around them again. Their breathing slowed. Flesh dampened with sweat cooled in the late-autumn air.

Slowly, Emily became aware of the forest—the creek running over a bed of gravel, turning the rocks one by one, smoothing and rounding them. The sound of lit-tle creatures scampering across the carpet of spruce needles and leaves, preparing their winter homes. The sway of treetops in a light breeze.

In a way she couldn't quite fathom, the granite rocks and virgin trees held the memory of others who had lain here together and loved. Voices from the past seemed to call out to her, but she couldn't quite make out their words.

She shivered.

"Someone walk over your grave, luv?"

"No. It's just that my mind seems to be playing tricks on me today."

"Hmm. Nice tricks, I trust." He nuzzled a kiss at the sensitive spot below her ear, then untangled himself from their embrace. "Best we get dressed or we'll both catch our death."

Emily tended to agree, although her shiver hadn't been related to the temperature.

Once they had their clothes on again, they sat on the blanket with their backs propped against the tree stump. Cal poured them each a glass of wine.

He lifted his glass in a toast. "To you, luv."

The look of love in his eyes curled through Emily, bringing with it the sensation of a summer day bursting with the scent of wildflowers and heavy with the heat of promise. "And to you, my love."

She sipped the fruity flavor. "Did you come here often with Alice?" she asked.

"It was not easy for us to find time to be alone together. Her father kept her under close guard."

"But you'd had experience escaping from tutors," she said with a smile, "so that hardly posed a challenge."

Crinkles formed at the corners of his eyes. "We managed as best we could."

Emily imagined so without feeling a single twinge of jealousy. "Did anyone else know of this spot?"

He sliced a piece of cheese and placed a bite between her lips, letting his fingers linger there for just a moment until she caught his flavor along with that of the snack he'd offered. A deliciously appetizing combination that stirred a hunger she thought she'd just fully satisfied.

"Not that I know of. We certainly did not tell her family. And at the time, there were no other houses out on Henderson Road. It seemed quite private enough for our needs."

Yes, a perfect lovers' trysting place. Very secret and secluded.

If all that Cal had told her was true—which Emily still couldn't quite believe—then Alice Henderson must have loved Calvert a great deal to risk the wrath of her father with secret meetings. From what Emily had seen of the wedding gown, she knew that love ran deep.

There was no possible way a woman like that would have betrayed her lover.

The next logical step to Emily's analytical mind was that Alice would have done everything in her power to leave a record that would save Calvert from the gallows.

Then where, Emily mused, would she have hidden a diary that would prove her lover innocent? Where would she leave a message before fleeing with her family? A family that suddenly "abandoned" their property, according to the census records.

Feeling restless, Emily stood. The breeze whispered against her ears. Secrets. Memories.

"What is it, lass?"

"I don't know. I think..." She walked to the edge of the creek and stared down at the silver thread of water. The boulders on the opposite bank marked the passage of time, an etched record of the wearing power of water on rock.

Not there. Not where the water might rise and wash it away.

Turning, she looked back to where Cal sat against the tree stump, his expression puzzled.

Buried treasure? she wondered.

The ground looked so hard it was difficult to imagine a young woman in a hurry trying to dig a hole. And if so, she would have left a mark, an arrow, something that would be a clue. Emily saw nothing at all out of the ordinary.

Except the stump next to which lovers lost themselves in each other's embrace.

As she walked back across the clearing, an odd sense of confidence buoyed her. It felt logical. She liked that feeling.

"What are you looking for?" Cal asked.

"The diary."

"Here?" He looked quite startled.

"You've searched the entire house without finding it. Where else would a young girl hide something like that besides the one other place she hoped you would think to look." Emily circled the tree stump, discovering an open scar left where a branch had broken off.

"It never occurred to me.... I have not been back here since I was hung. The memories were simply too painful. Her betrayal..."

Emily picked up a stick and poked at the matted leaves and dirt in the hole. The opening wasn't large, only a few inches across. "She wouldn't have thought of that because she knew she hadn't betrayed you."

"The court-martial tribunal certainly believed the major's story. So, I fear, did I," he said with a trace of sadness.

"You were all wrong."

Her stick touched something hard and unyielding. Something metal.

Excitement tightened her throat. "Cal..."

In an instant, he was beside her. "What is it?"

A mixture of fear, disbelief and expectancy flip-flopped her heart and stomach. "I think it's here."

Dropping the stick, she reached through the opening and dragged out a handful of dirt and leaves. The scent of decay tickled her nostrils.

"Here. Let me." His voice was husky with barely controlled emotion.

"No. I can get it." Though she didn't relish the feel of dirt and who-knew-what-else in her hands. "There's not much room in here. The opening's so small." Just right for a woman but a tight squeeze for a man.

She dragged out more dirt, and he tried to peer over her shoulder into the dark hole.

"Can you feel it, lass?"

"Not yet." She tried again. God, she hoped it wasn't an old beer can. The disappointment would shatter Cal.

Her fingers closed around the edge of a box. A metal box. Tin, she thought. She tugged, loosening more of the humus.

She fought off tears that suddenly stung at the back of her eyes. Alice's diary! It hardly seemed possible, and yet . . .

The box broke free. She slipped it from the hole.

Rectangular, the box was no more than six inches long by four inches wide and half that deep. Though most of the paint had dissolved away, the metal box looked like one of those that had been used to contain patent medicines—in the eighteenth century. A common relic found in any museum.

As she held out the box for Cal's inspection, her hands trembled. "Do you want to open it?"

"Dear God, Emily, I don't think I can." He swayed, his face drained of all color. "You do it."

Nodding, she licked her lips and forced herself to draw a steadying breath.

Slowly, she pried open the lid.

Chapter Thirteen

The leather-bound book looked fragile and aged and bore traces of the oil of human hands. Alice's hands?

With a single trembling finger, Emily lifted the cover.

Written on the first page in a fine, precise hand were the words *Given to Alice Henderson in celebration of her seventeenth birthday, 28 June in the year of Our Lord 1777.*

Emily expelled the breath she'd been holding. "The diary, Cal. It's really her diary."

"Quickly, lass. What does she say? Does she admit the truth? That I told her nothing?"

Easing the diary from its container, Emily noted a small leather purse tucked beneath it, but knowing how anxious Cal was, she decided to deal with that later. First she would have to read the diary.

She took the book to the blanket and settled down with her back against the stump. The paper was so old she was afraid the least little effort would tear it.

Running his hands through his dark hair, Cal paced around her. "Get on with it, girl. You've got me on needles and pins."

"I can't rush this. Let me just see . . ."

She skimmed quickly. The early pages seemed devoted to the everyday happenings on an eighteenth-century farm. Alice and her mother had spent two days canning fruit; her youngest brother Edgar had gotten into trouble by letting the cow out of its pen. His father had taken his belt to the boy, for which Alice expressed considerable sympathy, as a loving big sister would. She'd sneaked a piece of pie to him after he'd been forced to go without his supper.

Emily smiled, feeling connected across time. Her great-great-great-grandmother had been a kind person.

"By all that is holy, Emily. Tell me what she says." Cal's agitated voice echoed around the clearing.

"So far, she hates canning cherries and loves her little brother."

He muttered an oath. "But what of me?"

"She hasn't mentioned you at all yet." Emily turned the page. "When did you meet her?"

"My God, how can I remember at a time like this? The good name of Witherspoon is at stake." He marched across the clearing and back again, tempted, she knew, to yank the book from her hands, but even more fearful of what it might, or might not, reveal.

"It would help to know the time of year, Cal. All of these entries are dated."

He halted and stared off into the distance. "'Twas summer when I arrived. Bloody hot, with mosquitoes so thick you got a mouthful every time you spoke."

July or August. She carefully turned through the pages. Alice had gone to church in Honorville regularly and wrote of seeing her girlfriends there.

Emily's gaze skimmed a late July entry. Wings of excitement, like harried butterflies, fluttered in her chest as she read aloud. "'There was a new man at church today, a friend of Deacon Aldridge. He was quite tall and had very black hair, a wave of which tended to slide in a most attractive way over his forehead. His eyes were a shade of blue the likes of which I have not before observed. Like blue diamonds, I imagine as I think of him now.'" Emily glanced at Cal. An accurate description, though she hadn't thought of his eyes resembling diamonds. From now on, she would.

"'When he smiled at me,'" Emily continued to read, "'I had the strangest feeling low in my belly, like something quite exciting was about to happen, though I know not what.'" Emily had experienced exactly the same sensation with Cal—more than once.

"'Later I learned his name is Calvert Witherspoon and he is from England. I fear he is here because of the terrible war being waged, yet I still hope for a chance to see him again. Perhaps he will even choose to call on me though I have the feeling my father would not approve.'"

Emily leaned back against the stump. She fought the feeling she was invading Alice's privacy. Surely to have the diary found was what the woman had hoped.

"Sounds like love at first sight," she said nervously, glancing at Cal. "You seem to have that effect on us Henderson women."

Impatiently, he shrugged off her comment. "'Tis of no consequence now. 'Twas the springtime when the trouble began."

Continuing her hurried perusal of the diary, she found Cal's name taking on a greater prominence. It was like watching Alice falling in love, a journey Emily had recently made with the same man.

"Listen to this, Cal. 'My life grows more complicated by the moment. The people of Honorville are in support of the Crown. It is only we, the Hendersons, who pray mightily for the success of the new confederation and freedom from the oppression of King George. We must not let our views be known for surely we would be driven away. I have learned my own true love is a British Captain, teaching our neighbors to spy on those who would overthrow the King. From him I must keep this one dark secret and my heart breaks each time I must lie to him. For to tell him the truth, that my father and brothers actively oppose the King, would surely mean I would lose Calvert. That I could not bear.'"

"She should have told me," Cal said harshly, his jaw held at a grim line and a muscle tensing at his cheek.

"She loved you, Cal. And her family. Can't you feel how torn she was between her two loyalties? What else could she do?" What would she herself have done? Emily wondered, if faced with the same dilemma. Sometimes life didn't offer easy answers.

"Look at the final entries, lass. If she told the truth, it will be there."

Doing as ordered, Emily turned to the back of the book. Instead of a clear, precise hand, the writer's words on these last pages were a hurried scrawl that palpitated with frenzy.

"'Within days my beloved will die for a crime he did not commit. Somehow it is all my fault.'"

Cal groaned and collapsed on the blanket beside Emily. "All is lost...."

"Now just wait a minute. Have a little faith in a woman who loves you." She continued to read. "'Even as I write these words, my eyes are filled with tears and my heart is breaking. My hand shakes but I must tell the whole story. Major Hussey is prepared to swear Calvert told me everything, which cost British lives in an ambush. On my family Bible, I swear that is not true. Calvert told me nothing. He is far too honourable a man to reveal secrets to another.'"

"Aye. That is true, by God." Cal clenched his fist in the air.

"'I vouchsafed again and again to the major that I had no knowledge of British movements. Nor did my family. He badgered me unmercifully.'"

"The bastard!"

"'Yet he would not believe me. I can only think he is jealous of my beloved Calvert. For what reason, I know not.'"

"Because he was an ignorant lout and he knew just what I thought of him. It was probably the bloody sod himself who led his boys into a trap. The fool ordered them not to retreat even though they were outnumbered."

"Hush, Cal." She placed a calming hand on his arm and felt him tremble. "Let me finish."

"Aye." He covered her hand with his, his fingers unusually cold. "Let's hear it all."

"'I write these words in the hope my beloved will escape the hangman's noose and know to search for the truth in our secret meeting place—'"

"I didn't even consider—"

"'—for it is here my heart will wait for his return for as many lifetimes as it will take.'" Emily felt an odd shifting of her equilibrium. Had her ancestor somehow hoped a later generation would produce a woman, with a middle name of Alice, who would search out her lover? With a shake of her head, she put aside the unsettling thought, and continued reading.

"'We depart Honorville in haste, en route west to I know not where. In these last moments I shall endeavour to list the Honorville families who have betrayed the new republic, for it is they who must suffer the consequences of their actions. They, with M. Hussey, are planning an ambush of good and true N.H. troops who would fight for freedom. I fear great loss of life of our loyal lads.'"

"Ambush?"

"That's what she says. And I found an obscure reference to an ambush of New Hampshire irregulars at the library." At the time, it had seemed like a curious historical note, important only because it revealed there were spies in the neighborhood.

Following this last entry, Emily discovered a long list of names, virtually all of them familiar: Berrington, Pierce, Middleberry, Belinger. Every damn founding father!

Astounded, she said, "Do you know what this means?"

"They are all lads I employed—"

"Tories! Every one of them."

"Of course. This colony was quite loyal—"

"Cal, these people—their descendants—haven't been trying to run me out of town because of some ski resort development. They've been scared to death I'd find this diary with their names in it. That's got to be what's been happening."

He scowled. "But why? After all this time...how would they even know of the diary?"

"Beats me." She pulled the corner of her lower lip between her teeth. "Maybe on the way out of town, Alice gave them one last shot and let them know about the diary. To scare them, if nothing else."

"It's possible," he conceded. His hand had drifted to her shoulders, his fingers teasing lightly through the short hair at the nape of her neck. "She was a bit feisty now and again. Would be like her to try to get even."

More than possible, Emily suspected, even as she registered his gentle caress. She would have done the same.

It also might explain why Henderson House had been left so intact—and why Brady Berrington was so anxious for her to sell. Probably he was the one who wanted to buy it.

Turning one more page, she discovered a final note.

"'I pray you find this, my beloved.'" Emily's voice caught. She swallowed past the constriction in her throat, then continued. "'If so, use these coins I leave you to search for me. Others would call these my "30 pieces of silver'' for betraying the one I love. That is what M. Hussey would have you think. Trust in my love, my dearest. I shall wait for you—''' The mark at the end of the page was in the shape of a broken heart, one that looked very much like the split boulder on the far bank of the creek.

Falling silent, Emily wiped the tears away from her cheeks.

She could hear Cal's breathing, feel the warmth of his body along her side and where his arm rested across her shoulders. His unique musky scent clung to her, mixing with hers from their recent lovemaking. At that moment, she knew she and Alice shared one undeniable trait—their love for Cal, a priceless inheritance.

Calvert cocked one leg, rested his elbow on his knee and lowered his head to his hand. Two hundred years! At last he had the proof he had sought. In the end, Alice had not betrayed him. The relief he felt lifted a great weight from his shoulders.

He pictured his unyielding father standing before the hearth in the great room of the Witherspoon castle, his hands folded behind his back. He wore a somber black suit that matched his grim expression.

"Above all else," the man had warned, "while you are in the colonies, you must not bring disgrace to the Witherspoon name."

"I shan't, Father," Calvert had replied, feeling discomfited by the unfamiliar uniform he wore. "You have my word of honor."

A shudder shook Calvert at the clarity of his memory.

If his father, long since dead, could never learn the truth, at least now the record could be set to rights. The honor of the Witherspoon name. Calvert had not completely failed the man who had thought so little of him.

But at what price? he wondered, glancing at Emily.

"What are you thinking?" she asked softly.

"That you are the loveliest, most clever wench I have ever known." *And I cannot bear the thought of leaving you, for that would be worse than the lonely purgatory in which I have lived for so long.* "Who else would have thought to look in an old tree stump?"

Her smile brought a sparkle to her blue eyes. "Chalk one up to good genes. Or maybe all women think alike."

"Whatever the reason, I am grateful, luv." And filled with trepidation.

"The diary said something about coins." Emily lifted a purse from the metal box, handing it to Cal.

Puzzled, he loosened the drawstring and tipped a handful of coins into his palm. "'Tis but a few shillings."

"Don't be so sure." She examined one of the coins. "These are in practically mint condition. And look at the dates. I don't know much about coin collecting but I'll bet they're worth a whole lot more than their original face value."

"A few pounds, perhaps?"

She shrugged. "We won't know till we ask an expert."

Starting to put the remaining bread and cheese back in the wicker basket, she said, "Meanwhile, it's getting pretty late. I've got to get back before Becky comes home."

He helped her to her feet. Carrying the tin box under his arm, as well as the picnic basket and blanket, he retraced his steps on the narrow trail through the woods.

Emily followed him, her eyes focused on the box. Alice's diary.

Like a bolt, the full impact of what had happened in the last few hours struck her. Her knees went weak. She had to lean her hand against a tree to steady herself.

"My God, Cal...do you realize—" Her head reeled. It was as if someone had inserted a strange circuit board in her brain that no longer allowed her to logically process data.

He turned. "What's wrong, lass?"

"That diary. You." It wasn't possible. Two hours ago she had made love with a ghost? Hot, passionate, wild love. She'd breathed the air from his lungs as they'd kissed. She'd felt his muscle and sinew, relished his flavor and scent. Cal was human. Every one of her senses had confirmed that belief. Yet ... "Everything you've told me about being a—" she could hardly speak the word "—a ghost. It's true?"

"Aye. 'Tis true."

He wrapped his hand around her forearm to steady her. A firm, human grip. The hand he'd injured saving Becky. Flesh that had burned.

Emily felt a sharp throb at her temple, as though her brain was splitting in half. One side screamed, *He's not a ghost!* while the other told her it was true.

Her stomach turned queasy. "Maybe it's the wine," she mumbled. She simply wasn't thinking straight. Maybe she never would again.

"Let's get you back home and you can have a bit of a nap."

Emily didn't think a nap would help. All of the times Cal had appeared or disappeared without apparent reason played through her mind. A ghost could do that.

If that was the case . . .

Her thought processes plodded in slow motion.

If that was the case, then Cal's story about the dark tunnel—his out-of-body experience—was true, and the Keepers were real . . .

She closed her eyes as another wave of nausea swept over her.

Then that meant Cal would have to take the diary wherever he needed to in order to clear the Witherspoon name. He would then make good on his promise to the Keepers.

He would die.

Her hand flew to her mouth. She simply couldn't deal with that possibility.

FOR THE NEXT SEVERAL DAYS, neither of them mentioned the diary. By unspoken agreement, they weren't ready to face the full implications of their find. Cal had taken the diary and hidden it, she supposed, though she didn't know where.

Emily decided the situation was like waiting for that proverbial other shoe to drop. She didn't want to be the one to bring up the subject. Obviously, Cal didn't, either.

Instead, they made love each night with a bitter-sweetness that nearly broke her heart. Her chest ached constantly with the knowledge she was going to lose him. She just didn't know which day would be their last together. Nor did she truly understand why.

On Saturday they woke to a gloriously sunny day, one final gift from nature, Emily suspected, before winter set in for good.

She was in the kitchen washing out a paintbrush when Pete came racing into the room.

"Hey, Mom, there's a whole mess of cars and trucks and stuff coming up our driveway."

Lifting her shoulder, Emily brushed back a straying hair from her face. "Company? Now?" While she was dressed in her spattered paint clothes? Talk about lousy timing.

Drying her hands on a nearby towel, she went to find out what was happening.

Chapter Fourteen

Good heavens!

A whole row of trucks and cars filled the driveway. Dozens of laughing, shouting people spilled out of the vehicles, waving excitedly.

Emily had the distinct impression she was being invaded by an army of ants. Or that the whole town of Honorville had gone crazy.

What on earth . . .

Wearing khaki dungarees, Irene Carver appeared out of one of the lead cars, her good-looking son right behind her. The equally handsome man with her had to be her husband.

Emily hurried down the porch steps. "What's going on, Irene?"

"We're having a barn raising, New England-style."

"Barn?"

"Sure. Your carriage house."

"But why?" Since it wasn't insured, she hadn't expected to have enough money to restore the burned-out building for several more years. And had never considered . . .

Irene looped her arm around Emily's shoulder and gave her a hug. Her Cheshire cat grin was a couple of miles wide. "For what you did with the kids on the school bus. Most of these folks had someone on board. Sons. Daughters. Grandchildren. If you hadn't come along—"

"I only did what anyone else would have under the same—"

"Well, maybe they're feeling a little guilty you didn't get a better welcome to town."

Arching an eyebrow, Emily said, "You had something to do with planning this little surprise, didn't you?"

"So where's the crime?" She grinned again, the verdict admittedly guilty. "I like to take good care of my library patrons. Besides, in spite of my husband being a dry ol' anthropology professor, he's darn good with a hammer and saw. Got to keep the man out of trouble and he's already tired of my honey-do's."

With a self-satisfied smile and a vivacious bounce to her step, Irene pranced across the lawn to catch up with her friends. Several men were already unloading lumber while others had begun tearing down the remnants of the burned building. Kids were shoveling out the debris. Even the smallest child was busy with a broom.

The crisp morning air rang with the sound of hammers and the laughter of friends.

For a moment all Emily could do was stare in wonder. Then she heard Cal's voice behind her.

"What's all the ruckus?" He stood filling the doorway, his flannel shirt hanging open, a towel over his shoulder, and a streak of shaving soap still marking his sideburns.

She told him of the plans to rebuild the carriage house, amazement still filling her. "Looks like I'm finally getting welcomed to the neighborhood."

His lips quirked into a grin. "High time, if you asked me."

With the towel, he wiped the residual soap from his face. Emily wished she could have done that. He used a pine-scented foam that reminded her of secluded forest clearings and making love in the woods.

"Like I told you, establishing friendships anywhere takes time," she said.

He came to the edge of the porch, scanning the workers, a frown furrowing his forehead. "Is it all of the townspeople?"

"Not everybody, I suppose," she answered, wondering what he was worried about. "After all, the population's several hundred in town plus those of us on the outskirts."

"The families listed in the diary, lass. Are any of them here?"

"I didn't pay much attention..." She studied the crowd. "None that I recognize."

Calvert buttoned his shirt and tucked the tails inside his jeans. He didn't like the idea that none of the original families had joined in the welcome. For the last several days, it had troubled him mightily that Emily might still be in danger because of the diary. Under no circumstances could he leave Honorville while she was still at risk. Not that he wanted to leave at all.

"What's bothering you, Cal?"

"Just seems a bit odd, is all. 'Tis of little import." Not that he would share his worries with Emily. Though he had to admit there had been no problems of late, the possibility still remained. "I had best join them. See if I can lend a hand."

Puzzled, Emily watched Cal walk toward the carriage house. It did seem strange not a single founding family had showed up. But then, she wasn't sure she wanted them for friends, anyway. Their rudeness had left a bitter taste in her mouth. And if they were the source of the vandalism...

Irene Carver and the others were far more to her liking.

It seemed like no time at all before the framers raised the first wall, to the cheers of the crowd. The women in the group had provided do-it-yourself sandwich makings, mounds of potato salad and coleslaw. Very soon, however, it became obvious they were going to run out of cold drinks and beer.

Emily decided she'd go to town for more drinks. Maybe the makings for a tossed salad, too. She went in search of Cal, to let him know what she was up to. Excitement was in the air, and the spirit of friendship. Everyone seemed eager to talk to her.

Stephanie's mother pulled Emily off to the side.

"I don't like to impose," she said, "but we've been thinking about getting Stephanie a computer for Christmas. She's been begging for one. For her schoolwork, you know."

"I'm sure that would be good for her," Emily replied. She imagined that was one child who got almost everything she asked for.

"Well, the trouble is, my husband and I are so confused about what to buy. We have all the catalogs. Would it be too much to ask if I dropped by one day next week? Maybe you could explain. . . ." The short, stocky woman looked so concerned. "This computer business makes me feel so stupid."

"I'd be happy to do what I can, Vera. And you don't have to feel stupid. It's just new for you." She sensed the woman was offering friendship as well as asking for help. "I may even know of a couple of good sources for inexpensive computers."

Vera thanked her profusely, and Emily moved on, still in search of Cal.

A moment later, she was stopped again, this time by an older woman she didn't recognize.

"I just wanted to say how much we appreciate . . . Donnie was on the bus." The woman slipped a straying strand of gray hair back into the bun at her nape. "He's our only grandchild. I don't know what we would have—"

"Please. Don't even think about it. We all do what we have to." Thinking of her own grandmother, whom she had dearly loved, Emily gave the woman a hug. It simply seemed like the right thing to do and it made her feel warm all over.

Eventually she made her way to where Cal was working with the men framing the back wall.

"Drive those nails in at an angle, Cal," his co-worker was saying. "That way they won't come popping oot."

"Ah, I see," Cal replied, giving the nail several firm raps with his hammer.

"That's it. Now you've got the ideer." The two men exchanged knowing smiles.

Emily placed her hand on Cal's bent shoulder. He certainly had no trouble fitting in with the locals. The thought that they could live out their lives together here among friends brought tears of joy to her eyes. She simply wouldn't consider any other possibility.

"What is it, lass?" he asked, a smile creasing his cheek.

"I've got to run into town for soda and stuff. Keep an eye on the kids for me?"

"There are a dozen women cooing over Becky and pinching her cheeks," he pointed out, "and Pete has already decided on a career as a carpenter. They'll be fine, luv."

Unable to resist, in spite of all the people around them, she combed her fingers through the lock of Cal's dark hair that had drooped rakishly onto his forehead. At the moment she didn't much care what others might think. Her love for him was simply too strong to hide. "But you'll watch them?"

"Aye. I will not let them get into mischief."

Getting her car out of the driveway was a significant problem, but eventually she squeezed it past the parked vehicles without damaging any fenders.

She had just arrived at the grocery store and retrieved a grocery cart when Brady Berrington approached her.

"Afternoon, Emily," he drawled with a thick New England twang. "Saw you had a great crowd of visitors out your way this morning."

Emily gripped the cart handle more firmly. "Yes. My *friends* are helping me put up the carriage house again." And Brady wasn't counted among them.

"Do you think that's a good idea?"

"Of course it is. It's the kindest thing anyone has ever done for me."

His beady eyes narrowed. "Perhaps you haven't considered the long-term impact."

"Really, Brady, I'm not interested in discussing Henderson House with you at all." She tried to shove the cart past him, but he blocked her way.

"If you had a man to advise you, Emily, you'd know that your property taxes are sure to go up with a new building on your land."

"It's not a new building. It's the old one that burned down."

"The township may see it differently," he warned. "If you'd only let me—"

"Get off my back, Brady. I've had it with you and your cronies. No more threats and innuendos. And no more trying to undercut my profits, or cut off my electricity. In case you hadn't noticed, the town doesn't have any authority over me. I live in the county."

"You forget, Emily, the town council does have a certain amount of influence with county authorities. We have the interest of the entire community at heart. I do believe—"

She said a very unladylike word to shut him up. Anger and impatience heated her cheeks. Emily was going to dangle some bait in front of his narrow nose and see what kind of a reaction she got. "For your information, we've found a very interesting diary. All about the early years of Honorville. It seems Henderson women don't make idle threats.''

Brady sputtered. "I don't know what you're talking about."

"Don't you?" He sure as hell did. He looked like he was going to have an attack. "Then maybe one of your cohorts can enlighten you."

This time she did manage to get by Brady, leaving him standing stock-still in her wake.

Fuming, she grabbed several six-packs of soft drinks from the refrigerator section. The nerve of Brady and his gang of hoodlums. What on earth difference did it make after two hundred years that their ancestors had been Tories? It wasn't like they'd been spying for this week's number-one enemy.

In the produce department, she snatched up the makings for a salad almost without thinking. She had friends now. Good ones, too. The founding families could just stick that up their clannishness.

By the time she got home, the frames for two more walls were up on the carriage house and she'd calmed down considerably.

Watching the activities out the kitchen window, she tore lettuce for the salad, popping a bite of avocado into her mouth as she worked. While she quartered tomatoes, she finished consuming the first avocado, then peeled another one. They weren't quite as ripe as she would have liked, but they'd do—

Suddenly, she stared down at her hands and the single remaining slice of pale green fruit. She'd eaten nearly two complete avocados in the last ten minutes. Not one small bite had landed in the salad.

"Oh, no..." she groaned.

Twice in her life she'd gone on an avocado eating binge.

In an instinctive gesture, her hand covered her stomach. She searched her mind to remember the date. Her menstrual cycle was very regular. She was never late.

But she was now, she realized with a sinking feeling in the pit of her stomach.

"Dear God." She and Ted had always teased that Pete and Becky must have been the result of avocado seeds that she'd swallowed.

The possibility... the reality of her situation struck her like a slap to the face.

Pregnant! She fought back the scream that rose in her throat.

With poor timing that was characteristically male, Cal chose that moment to arrive in the kitchen. He slipped up behind her and gave her a quick kiss on the neck.

She whirled on him, jabbing him with her finger in the middle of his chest. "Haven't you ever heard of safe sex?" she cried.

His eyebrows formed a puzzled line. "Perhaps it is a new invention?"

Hysteria threatened. Good Lord, what was she saying? "Of course you haven't. I should have—" Her shoulders sagged. "Cal, I think...I think I'm..." with lips and tongue suddenly lacking basic coordination, she breathed out the word "...pregnant."

She watched as a series of colorfully conflicting emotions swept across his face. Surprise, disbelief, slow

acceptance, and finally the quirk of his lips and sparkle in his eyes reflected pure, unadulterated masculine
pride, as though he had accomplished this momentous
feat all on his own.

"You are breeding?"

She gritted her teeth. "We don't refer to it in quite
those terms anymore, Cal."

His expression softening, he took her gently by the
shoulders. "Ah, but it is the same, is it not? At last
there will be a true heir to the Witherspoon name."

"Is that all you can think about? Your damn family
name? What about me?"

He looked startled by her outburst. "You have born
two healthy children. Surely you do not fear child-
birth—"

"What I'm afraid of is being a thirty-five-year-old
single mother with *three* children to raise and a business to run. How in hell am I going to explain this to
the kids? And how about the neighbors?" With a
nearly frantic wave of her hand, she gestured outside
to the carriage house that was still crawling with her
new friends. "What on earth will they think?"

"Does it trouble you so much what others might
say?"

She turned away from him, burying her head in her
hands. Tears burned at the back of her eyes. She was
always so damned emotional when she was pregnant,
particularly in the first few weeks. Her stupid hor-
mones got all out of whack, bouncing her moods up
and down like a yo-yo. It was her own carelessness that
had gotten her into this fix. You'd think a woman her
age would know better.

"Is the thought of having my child so abhorrent to you, Emily?"

The rasping pain in Cal's voice made her lift her eyes to him. The hurt she saw cut painfully through her heart. "Oh, Cal . . . it's not that. . . ."

"It is so soon. Perhaps you only imagine—"

"I'm about as sure as any woman can be. I'm going to have your baby, Cal." Trembling, she opened her arms and stepped into his embrace. He smelled of sawdust and sweat. Very masculine. Very real. The man she loved. The man whose child she carried in her womb. She hadn't taken the time to think. . . .

A picture of that sweet-smelling baby came to her. A tiny head covered with soft, curling hair the color of midnight. Blue eyes gazing back at her—Cal's eyes. A wicked smile on the child's face that made her heart constrict with love. The smell of baby powder.

Not for a moment could she deny she wanted to hold that baby in her arms. Cherish him. Watch him grow into a fine, honorable man like his father.

"Yes, Cal, I want your child. I didn't plan it. If you'd asked, I would have said no. But God help me, I want your baby. Very, very much." Her shoulders settling, she sighed. "It's just that we have a few problems to work out."

The tension in his body eased, but he still held her tightly. "You are not sick, are you, luv?"

"No, I'll be fine. These days women are still safely having babies into their forties." Though she hadn't planned to be one of them. "There's a good hospital in Honorville. I'm sure I can find a doctor."

"Then there is nothing to worry about." He brushed a kiss to her forehead. His hand rested possessively on her hip. "The children will come around and be as eager as I for the babe. As for the neighbors..."

"Cal..." She palmed his face, feeling the rasp of afternoon stubble on his cheek. "We can't go on simply avoiding the issue. We both know you're going to have to leave me." Whether she understood it or not.

"No."

"You gave your word."

"It can wait. I won't leave you now."

"But, Cal—"

"I'm not going to discuss it, Emily. You are going to give me a son—"

"It might be a girl."

"—or daughter. I care not which. We will raise the child together, you and I. I've already made up my mind."

"The Keepers—"

"Beggar the Keepers! As long as you need me, I'm going to stay right here. They can wait another two hundred years, for as much as I care."

All that sounded too temptingly easy—and in direct opposition to Cal's strong sense of pride and honor. "Our child? The first Witherspoon in two hundred years. You'd have him grow up knowing the world thought his father had been hung as a traitor to his country?"

"We will not tell him anything about—"

"And if he decides to investigate his roots? Maybe travel to England to visit the family castle? Would you deny him that right, too? Children are very good about ferreting out anything you don't want them to know.''

"Emily," he growled. "That's enough. The decision is made."

She didn't think so. At the moment, however, she was too overwhelmed by the thought of being pregnant to argue. Her whole world had shifted on its axis.

A totally irrational giggle shook her. Impregnated by a *ghost?* That simply wasn't possible. At the very least, the news ought to make the *Gynecological Digest.* There'd be TV interviews. Maybe she could write a book. Famous, at last!

What if the baby could vanish like Cal? How on earth would she keep track of the child?

Oh, Lord. She was losing her mind. The men in the white coats were going to come haul *her* off in a minute.

Irene burst into the kitchen. "The guys are about to go on strike— Oops!" She halted by the door. "Looks like I interrupted a couple of lovebirds. Sorry."

Emily stepped away from Cal. She didn't bother to blush. Everyone would know soon enough that there'd been some serious goings-on at Henderson House. "It's all right. What's the problem?"

"Beer. Or lack of it." Irene eyed the two of them curiously. "But there's no rush if you've got something better to do."

"I just hope the walls go up straight with all the booze they're drinking," Emily said, smiling. She handed Irene a couple of six-packs and piled the rest in Cal's arms. Catching his eye, she felt a new rush of love sweep over her.

"I think they're sweating it off," Irene said with a laugh.

LATER THAT NIGHT, as Emily's head lay resting on his shoulder after their lovemaking, Calvert stared up at the ceiling. He ran his hand across her flat stomach.

His child. One they had made together. He had hardly thought it possible. Yet she was convinced it was so, and he could not find it within himself to deny it. Nor did he wish to.

She snuggled closer, her sweet scent teasing his nostrils, and sighed contentedly. "I saw Brady at the store today."

He scowled into the darkness.

"I told him we found the diary."

He nearly choked. "You *what?*"

"I said we found Alice's diary. I wanted to test my theory those jerks had been after the diary all along. I figured it would get them off my back."

A muscle rippled at his jaw. "What did he say?"

"He denied everything, of course. But I could see he was lying. I thought he was going to have a stroke."

"You should not have done that, Emily."

"Why not?" He felt her shrug. "After all this time, it doesn't matter."

It did to that Berrington bloke, Cal realized, and to all of the descendants of those he had employed against the colonies. He wasn't quite sure why that was so, but he knew Emily had placed herself at even greater risk by her revelation. All the more reason, he decided, he could not leave her.

Yet his conscience bothered him mightily.

After she had fallen asleep, her breathing regular and soft on his cheek, Cal slipped out of bed. He walked downstairs, found his pipe and lit it. Leaning his hand against the mantel above the cold fireplace, he slowly puffed the acrid smoke.

His child. What did he owe the seed that had sprung from his loins? he wondered. An untarnished name? Of that he was quite sure. But how?

And Emily. Dear God, how he loved her.

An ache tightened the muscles of his chest and groin as he thought of her. The scent of her hair. The soft, silky flesh of her body. The way her full breasts and hard, rosy nipples responded to his touch. The velvet folds beyond the bright patch of hair at the apex of her thighs. His back was still scored by the tender rake of her nails as she tightened around him.

She was so near, yet he felt her slipping away.

No man should be asked to leave such a woman.

Drawing again on the pipe, his thoughts shifted to his father. Lord Albert Witherspoon. A hard man. An honest man. Admired by many.

Calvert's memories were a mix of both love and hate for his sire. There had been no gentleness in the man. And for a lad who had been thrown into a role for which he was admittedly ill-suited, there were no excuses accepted for any small failure.

And fail, Calvert had. Through no fault of his own, perchance, but nonetheless his brief career on this earth had come to naught so far as his father was concerned. What a disappointment that must have been to the stern old man.

At this late date, what did honor require of him? he wondered.

To protect the woman he loved and their unborn child seemed quite clearly his first priority.

And then . . . the honor of his name. For the sake of that same child, as Emily had said, as well as easing his own conscience.

He was still mulling the possibility when he heard soft footsteps behind him.

"You can't sleep?" she asked, her voice laced with concern.

"I seek answers, all of which are difficult to accept."

"I know."

She came to him then, wrapping her arms around his waist and leaning her head against his chest, her short curls tousled from sleep. She wore the fluff of fabric he'd once bought for her, pink silk against her smooth flesh. It all seemed like such a long time ago. Or was it only yesterday? Time had such little meaning.

"I want the babe to carry the Witherspoon name," he said past the lump of acceptance in his throat.

"Of course. I'll make sure that's what the birth certificate says."

"Is that all that is required?"

Her head moved affirmatively against his chest. "What's your middle name, Cal?"

"Terrence. Calvert Terrence Witherspoon."

"That's quite a mouthful for a baby." Her voice quavered. "Terrence Morrell-Witherspoon. I'll call him Terry."

"And if it's a wee lass?"

She drew a shuddering breath. "Alice, I think."

"Aye."

He combed his fingers gently through her hair. Somehow he must remember her in exquisite detail— her shape, her touch, how she fit against him, and how she felt when he sheathed himself deeply within her.

"I want you to call Berrington." His voice was so thick the words seemed to fill his throat. "Tell him it is about the diary. I want to meet with all of those whose ancestors once stood with the Crown." Men he had recruited and to whom he owed a continuing allegiance, however poorly their descendants had behaved.

"There's no reason—"

"We will give them what they want. The erasing of history." Then, and only then, would Emily be safe. "After that, my luv..."

His words hung in the air a moment until Emily felt a hollowness filling her chest so deep and painful she knew she would never be whole again. It was as though her heart was being ripped away. She wanted to scream at him not to leave her, but she knew it wouldn't help.

"I know, Cal." In spite of her effort to be stoic, her chin trembled. "You don't have to say it. You're going back to Essex. To your home." To die.

"You were right this afternoon. When all is said and done, no matter that I wish it were not so, I have no other choice."

Chapter Fifteen

They came by ones and twos.

Brady and his equally narrow-faced mother. The old gentleman from the library, who turned out to be a descendant of Deacon Aldridge. Joshua Middleberry, the contractor. Sheriff Belinger. Mrs. Pierce from the drugstore and her arthritis-crippled husband, the longtime mayor of Honorville.

Each time a new guest arrived, a blast of arctic air swept through the hallway. Shrugging off their snow-dampened coats and hats, and leaving their winter boots by the front door, they crowded into Emily's living room.

As they all found places to sit, Emily stood with Cal in front of the fireplace. It made her a little sick to her stomach that these people had tried to drive her away from Honorville. For no good reason that she could see.

They were a somber group, as well they should be, she thought. Their secret was about to be exposed.

Studiously, they avoided looking at Emily—or at Cal in his full-regalia British officer's uniform. Only the sheriff took special interest in Cal's dramatic appearance. She wondered if he was remembering the night she'd asked him to search the house for a man dressed as a redcoat. A prowler she'd learned to love.

She hooked her arm through Cal's. Tonight, for as long as she could, she would draw on his sturdiness, his strength. There was substance to the man. More than most others had.

"Good evening, ladies. Gentlemen," Cal began, his voice firm and commanding. In one hand he held Alice's diary. The other was placed on the handle of his sword, for emphasis, Emily imagined. "For reasons that need not concern you, I have been searching for some time for this book which is now in my possession."

Every eye in the room shifted to the diary.

"It seems you, too, have been anxious to find this record of the past and were prepared to go to great extremes to acquire it."

Sheriff Belinger shifted uneasily in his chair.

"As you no doubt suspected, Alice Henderson, the author of this diary, named each of your families as supporters of the Crown during the war here in the colonies." Cal waited while they reacted to the confirmation of what they had no doubt expected. His diamond-hard gaze scanned the room.

Emily sensed that behind their blank expressions, the Honorville founding families were all sweating. Cal exuded so much authority it would be hard not to. Men would follow a man like that into battle, placing their lives in his capable hands. Whatever he might think, Cal had never failed those who had been loyal to him.

Somehow he would find a way not to fail her, either, Emily decided. She had to believe that. For the baby. And for herself, she thought, trying to ignore the band of pain that tightened around her chest.

"Before I go further," Cal continued, "we wish to know why the diary and its revelations are so important to you."

Feet shuffled on the carpet and several people cleared their throats. Eyes darted from one guilty party to the other.

"Oh, what the hell," Sheriff Belinger grumbled. "I know my reasons. I've been thinkin' aboot running for state office. That little book you got there would just muddy the political waters."

"Ah, ambition." Cal nodded. "A worthy motivation in any century."

"But I won't stand for any blackmail," the sheriff insisted, "if that's what you two have in mind."

Ignoring the accusation, Cal scanned the room again, settling his gaze on the mayor. "Do you, too, seek higher office?"

Mayor Pierce fingered an imaginary piece of lint on his trousers with his gnarled hands. "You just don't understand, young man. It's economics we're worried about." Next to him, Brady nodded in agreement and so did the mayor's wife. "If all of that were to come out, we might never again see a New Hampshire tourist in Honorville. Our ancestors cost the lives of a lot of young men from this state. Maybe no one from New England would ever want to come here again. We've got businesses to run. Property values would tumble. We simply couldn't risk—"

"Then 'tis greed at the crux of the matter." Cal turned to Middleberry. "Is that your reason, as well?"

"My folks always said that's what we was supposed to do. Find that fool diary."

"Better and better." Cal riffled to the back of the diary. "Now we have ambition, greed, and ... tradition." He laced his words with sarcasm as he ripped out a single page from the book. "On this page alone are your names listed and therefore 'tis the only bit of this book that concerns you. On that you will simply have to trust my word."

"We don't intend to tell anyone what we've learned," Emily said, "and even if the true history were known, I think you're wrong that it would make any difference to the local economy—or your political aspirations. Maybe two hundred years ago. But not now."

Cal wadded the single sheet of paper into a ball and tossed it into the fire. A red-gold flash shot above the other flames.

"Now I want your word," Cal said, "that you will no longer harass Emily Morrell."

The fire crackled in the silence. The room felt overly warm with so many people filling it, all of them suffering from nervous tension.

"Very well," the mayor finally agreed. "It's time to put this all behind us. You have our promise." He stared to ease himself from the chair with his cane.

"Wait a minute," Emily interjected. "Before you go, I have some questions I want answered."

Again the conspirators looked at each other nervously.

"I'd like to know which one of you blew up my transformer."

Middleberry shifted his cap in his hands. "We thought you wouldn't much like living here without electricity."

"I see." She'd never tell them how much she'd enjoyed those few days of peace and quiet with no childish arguments over which TV program to watch. "And the carriage-house fire? The one that could have cost both Becky and Cal their lives. Was that your doing, too?"

There was a chorus of no's.

"We never intended to hurt anyone," the sheriff said. "That really was an accident. I checked into it real close."

Emily blew out a sigh of relief. She wasn't sure she could have continued to live anywhere near these people if they had been that vicious and uncaring.

"And all the flak I got about a license?" she asked. "Mayor? Were you behind that?"

He cleared his throat and raised himself as straight in the chair as he could manage. "Perhaps I misused my influence with the county."

"I'll say!" Frowning, she switched her attention to Brady. "What was your role in all this?"

His narrow cheeks turned a ruddy color. "They thought perhaps I would be able to persuade you."

"By dating me?" How sexist could you get?

"I didn't see it as a sacrifice, Emily. You are a very... attractive woman and I had considered we might—"

Brady's mother silenced him with a sharp-edged glare.

Choking back a laugh, Emily thanked him for what she assumed was meant as a compliment, though his approach to women certainly left a lot to be desired.

The guests were still subdued as she showed them to the front door. Emily was quite sure they would never really be her friends. For too many years they'd lived as closely knit conspirators. They weren't likely to open up now.

Confident she was building her own set of friends, she didn't mind. The town was big enough for all of them.

She returned to the living room to discover Cal had turned down the lights, and soft music was playing.

"Dance with me, luv."

Her throat constricted. *Their last dance,* she realized. He was telling her goodbye. She'd known for days it would come. Still, it was too soon. It would always be too soon.

He bowed to her formally, his sheathed sword shifting at an angle.

On legs suddenly gone nerveless, she curtsied in response. Her heart was too busy breaking to let her feel foolish in her knee-length skirt, so contemporary compared to his uniform. They'd arranged for the children to spend the night with friends so there would be no interruptions in these last few hours they could spend together.

With outstretched arms, they reached for each other, as they once had in the cramped space of the attic. Her palm was damp against his; Cal's other hand was firm and steady at her waist while she rested a trembling hand on the epaulet at his shoulder.

Their eyes met and held. In that moment, Emily tried to imagine all that their future should have been—and lived it in the time it took for a dozen heartbeats. Their declaration of vows and undying love in a small church somewhere nearby, Becky and Pete in attendance. The birth of their child, soft and mewling against her milk-laden breast, Cal's smile filled with masculine pride. The passing years. Gray lacing Cal's dark hair as he grew older, the creases at the corners of his diamond-blue eyes deepening.

Dear God, why couldn't it be?

"Do you remember the first time we danced, luv?"

She swallowed the lump in her throat. "Yes." In a magical attic that was for a few minutes an imaginary ballroom.

"You thought me quite strange."

"I think I loved you even then," she admitted, her weak effort to lift her lips into a smile a dismal failure.

"The feeling came so quickly on us."

"Aye," she agreed, unconsciously adopting his manner of speech, as lovers so often do.

Still at arm's length, he began to move them gracefully around the room in time with the soft music playing on the stereo. The chairs and tables became laughing couples they circled, though there was no matching joy in Emily's heart. She closed her eyes and tried to will herself to think only of this one moment. It didn't work.

Her legs felt like someone had filled them with lead. The air felt hot, smoky, weighing down on her. Her lungs seemed unable to draw enough oxygen against the constriction she felt in her chest. Her breastbone ached.

"Cal..." Her chin puckered; her eyes stung with the burn of tears she didn't want to shed. Not now. "Oh, please. I don't think I can do this." *I can't say good-bye.*

"Dancing is not a hard thing to do. We have done it before."

Not a last dance. Not when her insides felt like they were being ripped apart.

"Let me show you..." she whispered, her voice catching. She slipped up closer and wrapped her arms around his neck, pressing her body against the length of his. "...how we slow-dance now."

His warm breath flowed across her cheek and his arms instinctively slid down her back to the swell of her hips. "I do believe this could be viewed as progress. A much more pleasant position for dancing than of old."

Calvert found himself swaying with Emily in his arms. There was no need to move his feet; the music became an unimportant sound that barely touched his awareness.

Instead his thoughts were centered on the way their thighs brushed together, the press of her pelvis against the rigid ache of his groin, and how the pressure of her breasts felt against his chest. He rested his cheek lightly on the silken strands of her hair, inhaling her sweet, citrus scent. Such fine, golden hair. Like sunrise streaking out over the ocean on a summer's day.

He would always remember her thus.

The hem of her skirt shifted rhythmically against his breeches, a whispering sound that came with each light brush of fabric on fabric. Her fingers at his nape knitted through his hair with a barely controlled urgency that repeated itself, twisting painfully through his gut.

He turned his head to kiss her and found eager, hungry lips meeting his. Savoring each moment, her willingness, his tongue discovered the sensitive flesh within her mouth. Velvet heat.

Emily uttered a low moan that tormented him with its mournful sound. By all that was holy, how could he leave this woman? Yet he must. Of all he had endured in two hundred years, that was the cruelest torture of all. Honor carried with it a high price.

Unable to breathe with the press of anticipated agony on him, Calvert rocked Emily in his arms.

"Cal?" she asked softly, her head at the crook of his neck.

"Aye, lass."

"I know you have to leave. But if..." Her voice broke. "If you can find a way, come back to me."

She had so much courage, he thought. Her bravery ran much deeper than his. "If it is at all possible, I shall return to you," he vowed hoarsely.

"Love me, Cal," she whispered, her warm lips searing the side of his neck.

"Always."

"Now. Here by the fire." She wanted to be as close to Cal as was humanly possible—to have their bodies meld into one, where there was no beginning and no end. Her breasts would mold against his broad chest, caressed by the crisp covering hair. Her legs would entwine with his, finally drawing him within her until she absorbed his essence and became a part of him as he had become an inseparable piece of her soul.

If she could not have eternity with this man, she would claim what she could. The memories she'd carry with her to the grave.

He undressed her slowly, though his hands trembled with the effort not to rush. As he bared each new bit of creamy flesh, he tasted her. A rich, satin flavor that had him hungry for more, and he knew that through all of time he would be a starving man without her.

Emily struggled to unbuckle the leather straps that crossed Cal's chest and the belt that held his sword. When the symbols of his office dropped to the floor with a soft thud on top of her discarded skirt, she removed the crimson sash at his waist and then concentrated on getting rid of any bit of clothing that would come between them.

They gazed at each other with love, as though to memorize each line, each curve and angle.

The firelight cast shadows across Cal's lean body, emphasizing muscle and sinew, the rippled flatness of his stomach.

"You're so beautiful," she said. So human, she thought as continued disbelief that Cal was anything other than a man rocked her mental equilibrium.

"It is you, luv, who is the beauty. I never shall forget."

She knelt before him, touching him with her hands and lips, to reassure herself that all of her senses still functioned as they should. His warm, musky scent flared her nostrils. Salt and sex registered on her taste buds and her hands measured the width and length of him. For Emily, Cal would always be a man. Her mind refused to accept any other alternative.

Groaning, Calvert knelt with Emily, then stretched her out before the fire. "I have never known such a woman as you. Nor have I wanted one more." The sensual play of firelight gilded her flesh a golden shade, shifting over her soft curves, each part of her body worthy of an artist's attention. Her hooded eyes were filled with deep passion.

He kissed the hollow at the base of her throat, letting his tongue linger a moment there while his hands caressed her breasts. Her nipples hardened at his touch.

He curved his hand to the shape of her midriff, her thigh, then explored the heart of her femininity. Gasping, she swayed against his hand.

"Easy, luv."

"I want to wait, Cal," she cried, the sob catching in her throat. "To make it last. But I can't...."

She moved beneath him, wrapping her arms around his shoulders and lifting her legs to circle his waist. Emily knew Cal could keep her safe in the world they created here. In these minutes together they would live a lifetime of love. They had to.

Strong hands raised her hips as he slid into her. The flexing of his powerful body was another kind of reassurance that he was real.

Emily's thoughts scattered and burst into a million sparks as he thrust deeply within her. She gave herself over to the moment. No past. No future. Only the incredible waves of pleasure exploding within her. Yearning fulfilled.

Clinging to him tightly, feeling the sweat of their bodies mixing, Emily felt a single tear slide down her cheek. She couldn't cry now. Not when she was so full of her love for Cal.

After the fire died down and the room chilled, they went upstairs together to make bittersweet love once again. Even as he filled her this one last time, Emily's heart cried out in denial. Her love. Her life. He was so much a part of her, she could not accept they would never be together again. Nothing in her experience had prepared her for the bleakness she knew she would have to face. Alone.

When she awoke the next morning, the scent of him was still on her flesh, his flavor in her mouth, her body warm from his caresses. Turning her head, she found the small leather purse with its ancient coins resting in the hollow of Cal's pillow where he should have been. An inheritance for their child, she thought, finally releasing the tears that she had held back.

EMILY HURRIED TO ANSWER the knock at the front door. Company always showed up at the darnedest times, she thought as she used an old rag to wipe at a paint smudge on her hands.

"Looks like I caught you at a bad time," Irene said from the other side of the screen door. "If you're too busy—"

"Don't be silly. Come on in." She shoved open the door. "I'm no busier than usual." Staying occupied was the only way Emily had kept at bay the lightless corners that had crept into her life these last few weeks. Desperate loneliness had replaced Cal. She fought the sensation, only to lose the battle she waged more times than not.

"Besides," she said, lifting her chin with new resolve, "I could use something to drink. How 'bout you?"

Agreeing easily, Irene followed her into the kitchen. "How's all the remodeling going?" She shrugged off her coat and draped it across one of the maple kitchen chairs.

"Slow but sure." Emily measured coffee into the filter for Irene and got a glass of juice for herself.

"Cal certainly seemed like a handy kind of guy to have around. I guess he's a lot of help."

Emily's hands stilled. "He's gone."

"Oh? I thought . . . It's none of my—"

"He had some business to attend to. In England." She turned and forced a smile to her lips. She discovered Irene's dark eyes gazing at her with sympathy and concern, easily able to read her false bravado.

"So he's planning to come back?"

"He said . . ." She swallowed hard. "He said he'd try."

"Have you heard from him?"

She shook her head, knowing that she would never hear from Cal again.

"Actually, I dropped by because . . . I hadn't seen either of you in town for couple of weeks. I got concerned."

"Concerned?"

Irene pulled a folded newspaper from her coat pocket. "Emily, do you take the Concord newspaper?"

Ignoring a ripple of anxiety that skittered down her spine, Emily retrieved a mug from the cupboard and placed it on the counter. "The papers pile up in the living room, and every few days I take them out to the recycling stack in the carriage house. I mean to, but I never seem to get around to reading them."

"I was afraid of that." She opened the newspaper to a back page. "There's a wire-service story here date-lined Witherspoon Castle, Essex."

Feeling the blood drain from her face and her knees going weak, Emily sat down heavily in a chair. "What does it say?"

"It's about... Oh, Emily, it may not mean a thing."

"Please."

She glanced at the paper and then back at Emily again. "An unidentified man died mysteriously at the gates to the castle. He was wearing an Honorville High jacket, and I'd seen the one Cal wore...."

Denial roared in Emily's ears.

"The odd thing is, this man had an old diary with him, and there's been some talk around town lately. Whisperings, you know. About ghosts and diaries. None of it meant anything to me." She shook her head. "According to the newspaper account, if authorities are able to authenticate the diary it would prove the last Witherspoon heir, a British captain who was hung as a traitor here in New Hampshire, was innocent of those charges."

Emily's hand covered her mouth. She squeezed back the threatening tears. He'd done it. Dear God, he'd cleared his name. The last act of an honorable man.

"This guy's name that they are talking about was Calvert Witherspoon. It seemed like such a strange coincidence. . . ."

"It's not a coincidence." Emily's voice rasped painfully in her throat. "It was Cal."

"You mean they were related?"

"No, I mean the man you met—Cal—" she steadied her voice "—*was* Calvert T. Witherspoon, captain in His Majesty's Own, hung as a traitor in 1778."

Irene looked incredulous.

"The ghost who haunted Henderson House for better than two hundred years," Emily explained, as though such a statement would make sense to anyone. It certainly didn't to her.

"Let me pour the coffee," Irene said, concern written all over her face.

"I didn't believe it, either—I still think I don't, much less understand how. Or why." She wrapped her hands around her glass of juice. "You must think I'm crazy."

"I think you're distraught. A man who was obviously important to you goes off, and now I show up with this strange newspaper story. Remember, it's entirely possible this man they found isn't Cal at all—"

"Sit down, Irene. Right now I desperately need someone—someone very logical—to talk to or I'm going to come apart at the seams. I can't do that because of Pete and Becky and . . ." her hand slid to her lap ". . . the baby."

"Oh, my . . ." Visibly shaken, Irene lowered herself back into her chair. She gripped her mug like it might fly away at the least provocation. "Talk away."

Emily told her everything. From the beginning. Sipping coffee, Irene listened intently. She nodded occasionally, as though she understood, but Emily knew that couldn't be true. No one could possibly comprehend such an incredible story.

Finally, Emily ended with, "I've never in my life believed in ghosts or anything supernatural. It just didn't make sense to me. And I assure you, Cal was about as warm—hot-blooded—as any man could be. Yet..."

Irene blew out a breath. "I don't know what to make of it, either. I'm certainly not superstitious, but I do know there are some things beyond our understanding."

"I feel like I need a remedial course in Logic 101." She laughed a weary sound. "This whole business simply doesn't compute. If I can't figure all this out soon, or simply accept it, I think my wheels are going to come off."

"I hate to add another broken wheel to your wagon, but there's something else you should know. From the newspaper article."

Emily raised questioning eyebrows.

"It says somewhere between the castle and the morgue, this unidentified guy they found...well, he disappeared. Or rather, his body did."

Chapter Sixteen

Emily waited.

Her waist thickened until she couldn't snap her jeans. She ignored bouts of morning nausea, and painted and wallpapered, and still she waited.

Cal was coming back to her.

She knew it with a frightening certainty. Why else had his body vanished? Not one of his optical illusions. Not this time.

But what was taking him so long? Where was that silver tongue of his that could persuade and wear down even the most stubborn opponent?

She'd thought it all through. If he could just manage to escape the Keepers one more time, she'd never let him go again.

Time after time, the creaking of the old house had awakened her in the night and she'd gone in search of Cal. His old room stood empty, the quilt folded at the foot of the narrow bed, the rocking chair unmoving. In the attic she found only memories. Sweet, tender and heartbreaking.

She'd return to her room, checking the closet where Cal had left his uniform. Running her hand along the heavy fabric, she thought of him. And tried not to cry. She *had* to hold on to her hope.

Then, one night as she sat staring into the fire, remembering how they had danced together, she felt a cold draft across her shoulders, and shivered.

"Hello, luv."

At the sound of his familiar voice, Emily's heart lurched against her ribs.

He stood near the bookcase, his thumbs hooked in his jean pockets, his maroon jacket hanging open. He smiled a crooked grin that made her feel all warm and wobbly inside until she realized a bright circle of light haloed his silhouette.

The tunnel, she thought, with momentary despair. No, he hadn't entirely escaped the Keepers.

"You came back," she acknowledged softly.

"Only long enough to say goodbye, I fear. 'Tis the best I could arrange."

She walked across the room. Her impulse was to throw herself into his arms. But a force she couldn't understand seemed to be in the way, as though a barrier had been erected that she couldn't cross.

"I don't want to let you go," she said.

"I know, lass." Tears glistened in his eyes. "You and the babe? Are you—"

"We need you, Cal. So do Pete and Becky."

"There is naught—"

"Do you love me?"

"Aye. You must never doubt that. I love you with all of my heart. Had I not already forfeited my life, it would be yours."

"Take my hand." She extended her hand, palm up.

"I am not sure—"

"Trust me, Cal. I have a plan."

He wrapped his long fingers around hers. His touch was as cold as a snowflake and equally insubstantial. The same icy feeling knotted in her stomach.

"If I talk to them, will the Keepers hear me?" she asked.

"I don't know. Certainly they listened to me until they grew quite weary."

"Good. Then I'll take up where you left off. Think of me as reinforcements." She dampened her lips with the tip of her tongue and drew a deep breath. Just how persuasive she could be in the next few minutes would set the course for the rest of her life.

"Keepers," she began politely, "I believe there's been a serious error made where Calvert T. Witherspoon is concerned. I don't know much about these things in whatever plane you exist on, but Cal isn't a ghost anymore."

The circle of light flared—with resentment, she thought. At least she had their attention.

"You see," she continued, "Cal shouldn't have been hung in the first place. He was totally innocent of all charges."

"I have used that argument with them, lass. They say they are not responsible for earthly mistakes."

"Just keep holding my hand and loving me," she urged. She had to believe their love was the most powerful force on earth—or anywhere else. It was their best, and only, chance to be together again.

The light made a threatening movement forward.

"Please, hear me out. By the time I met Cal, he wasn't a ghost. He simply couldn't have been. And I can prove it."

For a moment, the light wavered hesitantly.

"For instance," she went on hurriedly, "ghosts certainly can't injure themselves. That seems pretty obvious. Yet Cal did. He did something very brave and burned his hand. Can you concede that shouldn't have happened?"

Emily detected a distinct dimming of at least part of the light. Odd. Perhaps there was more than one Keeper. She also thought Cal's hand had grown warmer in hers, but she couldn't be sure.

"Then Cal found he couldn't walk through walls, or vanish when he wanted to. That's certainly a strong indicator he was no longer a ghost, if indeed he ever had been."

No reaction from the light.

"The fact that Cal also managed to get drunk lends further credence that there has been an error. As you no doubt know, drunkenness is directly related to the blood alcohol content. It's unreasonable to assume they are making red-blooded ghosts these days." Emily thought a little humor might help.

"There was my jealousy, too," Cal added, catching on to her line of reasoning. "At one point I was ready to throttle that Berrington bloke with my bare hands. The sensation quite startled me."

"That's right," Emily agreed, feeling his hand taking on more substance. "And it was because Cal loved me that he felt an emotion that surely isn't characteristic of ghosts."

"More than that, we *made* love, you and I." His gaze caressed her softly, intimately. "We did it bloody well and bloody often, it seems to me. I had been quite sure ghosts couldn't *do* that until you came along."

She lifted his hand. The light smattering of hair on the back of his hand felt rough against her cheek.

Again, the light faded slightly.

Now was the time for her final argument. The indisputable fact of Cal's humanity.

"Keepers, if you don't already know, you should be aware I am pregnant. It's Cal's child, of course. Then it follows—" she felt like she was driving home a point with Cal's sword, which was still in his room upstairs "—that Cal is human and should be with me and his unborn child."

Her words hung in the air.

The light pulsated, vacillating at first brightly and then with less intensity.

"Cal, come to me," she said in a hoarse whisper.

He did. He wrapped his muscular arms around her, and she caught the residual scent of his pine-soap shaving cream mixing with his thoroughly masculine aroma. Resting her head on his shoulder, she watched the light.

When it steadied into a low glow, she spoke again. "As I see it, you must give Cal back his life. Let him live out the rest of his years in the normal course of things."

Hovering, the light shrank.

"Kiss me, Cal." She was so scared, she trembled. She'd done all she could. Now it was up to the Keepers.

Cal's mouth covered hers in a hot, hungry kiss, his tongue probing and tasting. He pulled her hard against his chest.

For a long time he simply savored the feel of his woman, the way she seemed to fit against him. The Keepers couldn't deny what they could see with their own eyes. They were two humans in love.

When Cal and Emily looked again, breathless from their kiss, they stood alone in the darkness of the living room, the fire reduced to glowing coals.

Love was a potent and powerful feeling between two people.

The light was gone.

A WEEK LATER Cal and Emily became husband and wife as they took their vows at the Honorville church.

Pete and Becky were there, as well as Irene and a few townspeople.

"We shall grow old together, my love," Cal said. "And if you should precede me in death, wait for me in the tunnel. For I shall be there soon and we will be together forever."

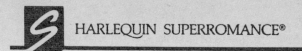

HARLEQUIN SUPERROMANCE®

HARLEQUIN SUPERROMANCE NOVELS WANTS TO INTRODUCE YOU TO A DARING NEW CONCEPT IN ROMANCE . . .

WOMEN WHO DARE!
Bright, bold, beautiful . . .
Brave and caring, strong and passionate . . .
They're women who know their own minds
and will dare anything . . .
for love!

One title per month in 1993, written by popular Superromance
authors, will highlight our special heroines as they face unusual,
challenging and sometimes dangerous situations.

Love blooms next month with:
#553 LATE BLOOMER by Peg Sutherland
Available in June wherever Harlequin Superromance novels are sold.

WIN-A-FORTUNE
OFFICIAL RULES • MILLION DOLLAR SWEEPSTAKES
NO PURCHASE OR OBLIGATION NECESSARY TO ENTER

To enter, follow the directions published. **ALTERNATE MEANS OF ENTRY:** Hand-print your name and address on a 3"×5" card and mail to either: Harlequin Win-A-Fortune, 3010 Walden Ave., P.O. Box 1867, Buffalo, NY 14269-1867, or Harlequin Win A Fortune, P.O. Box 609, Fort Erie, Ontario L2A 5X3, and we will assign your Sweepstakes numbers (Limit: one entry per envelope). For eligibility, entries must be received no later than March 31, 1994 and be sent via 1st-class mail. No liability is assumed for printing errors or lost, late or misdirected entries.

To determine winners, the sweepstakes numbers on submitted entries will be compared against a list of randomly preselected prizewinning numbers. In the event all prizes are not claimed via the return of prizewinning numbers, random drawings will be held from among all other entries received to award unclaimed prizes.

Prizewinners will be determined no later than May 30, 1994. Selection of winning numbers and random drawings are under the supervision of D.L. Blair, Inc., an independent judging organization whose decisions are final. One prize to a family or organization. No substitution will be made for any prize, except as offered. Taxes and duties on all prizes are the sole responsibility of winners. Winners will be notified by mail. Chances of winning are determined by the number of entries distributed and received.

Sweepstakes open to persons 18 years of age or older, except employees and immediate family members of Torstar Corporation, D.L. Blair, Inc., their affiliates, subsidiaries and all other agencies, entities and persons connected with the use, marketing or conduct of this Sweepstakes. All applicable laws and regulations apply. Sweepstakes offer void wherever prohibited by law. Any litigation within the province of Quebec respecting the conduct and awarding of a prize in this Sweepstakes must be submitted to the Régies des Loteries et Courses du Quebec. In order to win a prize, residents of Canada will be required to correctly answer a time-limited arithmetical skill-testing question. Values of all prizes are in U.S. currency.

Winners of major prizes will be obligated to sign and return an affidavit of eligibility and release of liability within 30 days of notification. In the event of non-compliance within this time period, prize may be awarded to an alternate winner. Any prize or prize notification returned as undeliverable will result in the awarding of the prize to an alternate winner. By acceptance of their prize, winners consent to use of their names, photographs or other likenesses for purposes of advertising, trade and promotion on behalf of Torstar Corporation without further compensation, unless prohibited by law.

This Sweepstakes is presented by Torstar Corporation, its subsidiaries and affiliates in conjunction with book, merchandise and/or product offerings. Prizes are as follows: Grand Prize—$1,000,000 (payable at $33,333.33 a year for 30 years). First through Sixth Prizes may be presented in different creative executions, each with the following approximate values: First Prize—$35,000; Second Prize—$10,000; 2 Third Prizes—$5,000 each; 5 Fourth Prizes—$1,000 each; 10 Fifth Prizes—$250 each; 1,000 Sixth Prizes—$100 each. Prizewinners will have the opportunity of selecting any prize offered for that level. A travel-prize option if offered and selected by winner, must be completed within 12 months of selection and is subject to hotel and flight accommodations availability. Torstar Corporation may present this sweepstakes utilizing names other than Million Dollar Sweepstakes. For a current list of all prize options offered within prize levels and all names the Sweepstakes may utilize, send a self-addressed stamped envelope (WA residents need not affix return postage) to: Million Dollar Sweepstakes Prize Options/Names, P.O. Box 7410, Blair, NE 68009.

For a list of prizewinners (available after July 31, 1994) send a separate, stamped self-addressed envelope to: Million Dollar Sweepstakes Winners, P.O. Box 4728, Blair NE 68009.

SWP-H493

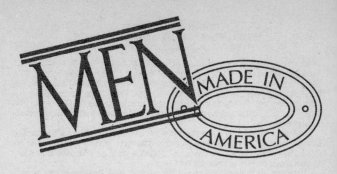

Fifty red-blooded, white-hot, true-blue hunks from every State in the Union!

Beginning in May, look for MEN MADE IN AMERICA! Written by some of our most popular authors, these stories feature fifty of the strongest, sexiest men, each from a different state in the union!

Two titles available every other month at your favorite retail outlet.

In May, look for:

FULL HOUSE by Jackie Weger (Alabama)
BORROWED DREAMS by Debbie Macomber (Alaska)

In July, look for:

CALL IT DESTINY by Jayne Ann Krentz (Arizona)
ANOTHER KIND OF LOVE by Mary Lynn Baxter (Arkansas)

You won't be able to resist MEN MADE IN AMERICA!